Homo

The Secrets of Auricular Confession

Anatiposi

Homo

The Secrets of Auricular Confession

Reprint of the original, first published in 1871.

1st Edition 2023 | ISBN: 978-3-38212-668-1

Anatiposi Verlag is an imprint of Outlook Verlagsgesellschaft mbH.

Verlag (Publisher): Outlook Verlag GmbH, Zeilweg 44, 60439 Frankfurt, Deutschland
Vertretungsberechtigt (Authorized to represent): E. Roepke, Zeilweg 44, 60439 Frankfurt, Deutschland
Druck (Print): Books on Demand GmbH, In de Tarpen 42, 22848 Norderstedt, Deutschland

THE

SECRETS

OF

Auricular Confession

EXPOSED!

IN THE

ORIGINAL LATIN,

AND TRANSLATED INTO

English and German,

FOR THE USE OF

FATHERS, HUSBANDS & BROTHERS,

BY HOMO.

Stereotype Edition.

1871.

Price Fifty Cents.

EXTRACTS

FROM

PETER DENS'

—AND—

BISHOP KENRICK'S

MORAL THEOLOGY.

Translated into

ENGLISH AND GERMAN,

For the use of

FATHERS, HUSBANDS, AND BROTHERS.

BY HOMO.

CHICAGO:
STEREOTYPE EDITION.
1871

PREFACE.

To the Reader:

You are here presented with extracts from Theological works of the Romish Church, published and circulated with the approbation of Councils, and Bishops, and taught as *Moral Theology* in the United States, and elsewhere—in the Nineteenth Century. Under each extract may be found the volume and page from which it has been selected. The Latin extracts are from *approved* Catholic Theology. The accompanying translations are for the people.

At a meeting of the Roman Catholic Prelates of Ireland, held on the 14th of Sept., 1808, it was unanimously agreed that *Dens' Complete Body of Theology* was the *best book* on the subject that could be published.

This resolution was subsequently confirmed by another, passed unanimously at a meeting of Roman Catholic Bishops, held in Dublin on the 25th of Feb., 1810, viz.:

"Resolved, That we do hereby confirm and declare our unaltered adherence to the Resolutions unanimously entered into at our last general meeting, on the 14th Sept., 1808."—*Wyse's Hist. Cat. Ass.,* vol. 2, Appen. p. 20.

The Archbishop of St. Louis, Missouri, endorses the Moral Theology of Peter Dens, as may be seen by reference to files of St. Louis papers of Feb., 1850.

It is presumed that Fathers, Husbands and Brothers may, with propriety investigate the *Moral Theology* which the Romish Priesthood are authorized to teach their wives   daughters and sisters in the Confessional.

2

Vorwort.

An die Leser.

Es werden ihnen hier Auszüge aus Theologischen Werken der Römischen Kirche präsentirt, die mit der Approbation von Concilien und Bischöfen veröffentlicht und die in den Vereinigten Staaten und anderwärts als Moralische Theologie gelehrt werden im neunzehnten Jahrhundert! Unter jedem Auszuge ist der Band und die Seite zu finden, von welchem derselbe entnommenen ist.

Bei einer Versammlung der römisch-katholischen Prälaten von Irland, abgehalten am 14. Sept. 1808, vereinigte man sich einstimmig dahin, daß Den vollständiges Werk über Theologie das beste Buch über diesen Gegenstand sei, das neuaufgelegt werden könnte.

Dieser Beschluß wurde später durch einen weiteren bestätigt, der bei einer Versammlung römisch-katholischer Bischöfe in Dublin am 25. Februar 1810 einstimmig angenomm wurde, dahin gehend:

"Beschlossen, daß wir hiermit bestätigen und erklären unsere unveränderte Anhänglichkeit an die einstimmigen Beschlüsse unserer letzten General-Versammlung vom 14. Sep. 1808."—Wyse's Hist. Cat. Ass. vol. 2. Appen. p. 20.

Der Erzbischof von St. Louis, Mo., indorsirte die Moralisches Theologie des Peter Dens, wie nachweislich der St. Louis Blätter vom Febr. 1850 ersehen werden kann.

Es wird vorausgesetzt, daß Väter, Ehemänner und Brüder werden mit Anstand, die Moralische Theologie prüfen, welche die Römische Priesterschaft ihre Weiber, Töchter und Schwestern im Beichtstuhl zu lehren autorisirt ist.   3   VOX POPULI.

A POPISH BULL, OR CURSE,

PRONOUNCED ON REV. WM. HOGAN, FORMERLY A PAPAL PRIEST
IN PHILADELPHIA.

" 'By the authority of God Almighty, the Father, Son, and Holy
Ghost, and the undefiled Virgin Mary, mother and patroness of our
Savior, and of all celestial Virtues, Angels, Archangels, Thrones,
Dominions, Powers, Cherubim and Seraphim, and of all the Holy
Patriarchs, Prophets, and of all the Apostles and Evangelists, of the
Holy Innocents, who in the sight of the Holy Lamb are found worthy
to sing the new song of the Holy Martyrs and Holy Confessors, and
of all the Holy Virgins, and of all Saints together with the Holy
elect of God;'—May he, William Hogan, be damned. We excom-
municate and anathematize him from the threshold of the Holy
Church of God Almighty: We sequester him, that he may be tormented, disposed and be delivered over with Dathan and Abiram, and
with those who say unto the Lord, 'Depart from us, we desire none
of thy ways;' as a fire is quenched with water, so let the light of him
be put out for evermore, unless it shall repent him and make satisfaction. Amen.

"May the Father, who creates man, curse him!—May the Son,
who suffered for us, curse him!—May the Holy Ghost, who is poured
out in baptism, curse him!—May the Holy Cross, which Christ for
our salvation, triumphing over his enemies, ascended, curse him!

"May the Holy Mary, ever virgin and mother of God, curse him!—
May St. Michael, the Advocate of the Holy Souls, curse him!—
May all the Angels, Principalities and Powers, and all Heavenly
Armies, curse him!—May the glorious band of the Patriarchs and
Prophets curse him!

"May St. John the Precursor, and St. John the Baptist, and St.
Peter, and St. Paul, and St. Andrew, and all other of Christ's Apostles together, curse him! and may the rest of the Disciples and
Evangelists, who by their preaching converted the universe, and the
holy and wonderful company of Martyrs and Confessors, who by their

4

works are found pleasing to God Almighty;—May the holy choir of the Holy Virgins, who for the honor of Christ, have despised the things of the world, damn him! May all Saints from the beginning of the world to everlasting ages, who are found to be beloved of God, damn him!

"May he be damned wherever he be, whether in the house or in the alley, in the woods, or in the water, or in the Church! May he be cursed in living and dying!

"May he be cursed in eating and drinking, in being hungry, in being thirsty, in fasting and sleeping, in slumbering and in sitting, in living, in working, in resting, and ***** and in blood letting!

"May he be cursed in all the faculties of his body!

"May he be cursed inwardly and outwardly! May he be cursed in his hair; cursed be he in his brains and his vertex, in his temples, in his eyebrows, in his cheeks, in his jaw-bones, in his nostrils, in his teeth and grinders, in his lips, in his shoulders, in his arms, in his fingers!

"May he be damned in his mouth, in his breast, in his heart. and purtenances, down to the very stomach!

"May he be cursed in his ***** and his ****; in his thighs, in *******, and his *** and in his knees, his legs, and his feet, and toe nails!

"May he be cursed in all his joints and articulation of the members; from the crown of his head to the soles of his feet may there be no soundness!

"May the Son of the living God, with all the glory of his majesty, curse him! and may Heaven, with all the powers that move therein, rise up against him, and curse and damn him, unless he repent and make satisfaction. Amen! So be it. Be it so, Amen!"

Eine Päpstliche Bulle,

oder Fluch,

Ausgesprochen über den Ehrw. Wm. Hogan, vormals päpstlicher
Priester in Philadelphia.

„Durch die Kraft Gottes, des Allmächtigen, des Vaters, Sohnes und Heiligen
Geistes, und der reinen Jungfrau Maria, der Mutter und Patronin unseres Heilan=
des, und aller himmlischen Kräfte, Engel, Erzengel, Throne, Herrschaften, Cherubim
und Seraphim; und aller heiligen Patriarchen, Propheten und aller Apostel und
Evangelisten, der heiligen Unschuldigen, die würdig erfunden worden sind, vor dem
Angesichte des Lammes zu singen den neuen Gesang der heiligen Blutzeugen und der
heiligen Bekenner des Glaubens und aller heiligen Jungfrauen und aller Heiligen
sammt den Auserwählten Gottes soll er, Wilhelm Hogan, verdammt sein. Wir ex=
communiciren und verbannen ihn von der Schwelle der heiligen Kirche des Allmäch=
tigen Gottes. Wir sondern ihn ab, daß er gepeinigt, überantwortet und überliefert
werde mit Dathan und Abiram und mit denen, die sagen zu dem Herrn: „Weiche von
uns, wir begehren deiner Wege nicht.“ Wie ein Feuer mit Wasser gelöscht wird, so
lasset sein Licht ausgelöscht sein für immer, wenn er nicht Buße thut und Genugthu=
ung leistet. Amen!

Möge der Vater, der den Menschen erschafft, ihn verfluchen!—Möge der Sohn, der
für uns gelitten hat, ihn verfluchen!—Möge der Heilige Geist, der ausgegossen wird
in der Taufe, ihn verfluchen!—Möge das heilige Kreuz, das Christus über seine
Feinde triumphirend bestiegen hat, ihn verfluchen!

Möge die heilige Maria, ewig Jungfrau und Mutter Gottes, ihn verfluchen! —
Möge der heilige Michael, der Fürsprecher der heiligen Seelen, ihn verfluchen!—Mö=
gen alle Engel und Fürstenthümer und Gewalten und alle himmlischen Heerschaaren
ihn verfluchen—Möge die glorreiche Schaar der Patriarchen und Propheten ihn ver=
fluchen!

Möge St. Johannes, der Vorläufer, und St. Johannes, der Täufer, und St. Pe=
ter und St. Paul und St. Andreas sammt allen andern Aposteln Christi ihn mitein=
ander verfluchen! Und mögen alle übrigen Jünger und Evangelisten, die durch ihre
Predigt die Welt bekehrt, und die heilige und wunderbare Schaar der Märtyrer und
Blutzeugen, die durch ihre Werke bei Gott, dem Allmächtigen, angenehm erfunden
worden sind;—möge der Chor der heiligen Jungfrauen, die für die Ehre Christi die
Dinge der Welt verachtet haben, ihn verdammen! Mögen alle Heiligen von Anfang
der Welt bis in ewige Zeiten, die als die Geliebten Gottes erfunden worden, ihn
verdammen!

Möge er verdammt sein, wo immer nur er sich befinde, ob zu Hause oder auf der
Gasse, oder im Walde, oder auf dem Wasser, oder in der Kirche! Möge er im Leben
und im Tode verflucht sein!

Möge er verflucht sein im Essen und im Trinken, in Hunger und in Durst, im Fasten und im Schlafen, Schlummern, und im Niederlassen, Wohnen, Arbeiten, Ruhen, und ***** und im Aderlaß!

Möge er verflucht sein in allen seinen körperlichen Fähigkeiten!

Möge er innen und außen verflucht sein! Möge er in seinen Haaren verflucht sein! verflucht sein in seinem Gehirn und in seinem Wirbel, in seinen Schläfen und in seinen Augenbrauen, in seinen Wangen, in seinen Kinnbacken, in seinen Nasenlöchern, in seinen Zähnen und Backenzähnen, in seinen Lippen, in seinen Schultern, in seinen Armen, in seinen Fingern!

Möge er in seinem Munde verdammt sein, in seiner Brust, seinem Herzen und Geschlinge hinab bis zum Magen selbst!

Möge er verdammt sein in seinen ***** und in seinen *****; in seinen Lenden, in seinen ***** und in seinen ***** und in seinen Knien, seinen Beinen und seinen Füßen und Fußnägeln!

Möge er verflucht sein in allen seinen Gelenken und Gliedern; vom Scheitel bis zur Fußsohle möge nichts Gesundes an ihm sein!

Möge der Sohn des lebendigen Gottes mit aller Herrlichkeit seiner Macht ihn verfluchen! Und möge der Himmel mit allen Kräften, die sich darin bewegen, sich gegen ihn erheben und ihn verfluchen und verdammen, wenn er nicht Buße thut und Genugthuung gibt! Amen! So sei es! Sei es so! Amen!" --

The following is the oath taken by every popish bishop on his consecration. It was abbreviated in compliance with a request from this country, by the Pope in 1846, but nothing in sentiment or spirit was omitted:

ROMISH BISHOP'S OATH.

"I, G. N., elect of the Church of N., from henceforth will be faithful and obedient to St. Peter the Apostle, and to the holy Roman Church, and to our lord, the lord N. Pope N. and to his successors canonically coming in. I will neither advise, consent, nor do anything that they may lose life or member, or that their persons may be seized or hands anywise laid upon them, or any injuries offered to them, under any pretence whatsoever. The Counsel which they shall intrust me withal, by themselves, their messengers or letters, I will not knowingly reveal to any, to their prejudice. I will help them to defend and keep the Roman Papacy and the royalties of St. Peter, saving my order against all men. The legate of the Apostolic foe, going and coming I will honorably treat, and help in his necessities. The rights, honors, and privileges, and authority of the holy Roman Church, of our lord the Pope and his aforesaid successors, I will endeavor to preserve, defend, increase and advance. I will not be in any council, action, or treaty, in which shall be plotted against our said lord, and the said Roman Church, anything to the hurt or prejudice of their persons, right, honor, state or power; and if I shall know any such thing to be treated or agitated by any whomsoever, I will hinder it all that I can; and as soon as I can, will signify it to our said lord, or to some other, by whom it may come to his knowledge. The rules of the Holy Fathers, the Apostolic decrees, ordinances, or disposals, reservations, provisions and mandates, I will observe with all my might, and cause to be observed by others. Heretics, schismatics, and rebels to our said lord, or his aforesaid successors, I will to the utmost of my power persecute and oppose. I will come to a council when I am called, unless I be hindered by a canonical impediment. I will by myself in person, visit the threshold of the Apostles every three years; and give an account to our lord and his aforesaid successors, of all my pastoral office, and of all things anywise belonging to the state of my Church, to the discipline of my clergy and people, and lastly to the salvation of souls committed to my trust; and will in like manner, humbly receive and diligently execute the Apostolic commands. And if I be detained by a lawful impediment,

I will perform all the things aforesaid by a certain messenger hereto specially empowered, a member of my Chapter or some other in ecclesiastical dignity, or else having a parsonage ; or in default of these, by a priest of the diocese ; or in default of one of the clergy, (of the diocese,) by some other secular or regular priest of approved integrity and religion, fully instructed in all things above mentioned. And such impediment I will make out, by lawful proofs, to be transmitted by the aforesaid messenger, to the Cardinal proponent of the holy Roman Church, in the Congregation of the sacred Council. The possessions belonging to my table I will neither sell nor give away, nor mortgage, nor grant anew in fee, nor anywise alienate, no not even with the consent of the Chapter of my Church, without consulting the Roman Pontiff. And if I shall make any alienation, I will thereby incur the penalties contained in a certain Constitution put forth about this matter.

"So help me God and these holy Gospels of God."

A large portion of the popish priests in this country are from Maynooth College, in Ireland. The following is the oath taken by them on being admitted to the order of priests :

ROMISH PRIEST'S OATH.

"I, A. B., do acknowledge the ecclesiastical power of his holiness and the mother Church of Rome, as the chief Head and matron above all pretended churches throughout the whole earth ; and that my zeal shall be for St. Peter and his successors, as the founder of the true and ancient Catholic faith, against all heretical kings, princes, states or powers, repugnant unto the same ; and although I, A. B., may follow, in case of persecution, or otherwise to be heretically despised, yet in soul and conscience I shall hold, aid, and succor the mother Church of Rome, as the true, ancient, and apostolic church ; I, A. B., further do declare not to act or control any matter or thing prejudicial unto her, or her sacred orders, doctrines, tenets, or commands, without leave of its supreme power or its authority, under her appointed, or to be appointed ; and being so permitted, then to act, and further her interests more than my own earthly good and earthly pleasure, as she and her Head, his Holiness, and his successors have, or ought to have, the supremacy over all kings, princes, estates, or powers whatsoever, either to deprive them of their crowns, scepters, powers, privileges, realms, countries, or governments, or to set up others in lieu thereof, they dissenting from the mother church and her commands."

Many Jesuits are in this country; and their number is rapidly multiplying. The following is the oath they take on joining the order:

THE JESUIT'S OATH.

I, A. B., now in the presence of Almighty God, the blessed Virgin Mary, the blessed Michael the Archangel, the blessed St. John the Baptist, the holy apostles St. Peter and St. Paul, and all the saints and sacred host of heaven, and to you my ghostly father, do declare from my heart, without mental reservation, that his Holiness Pope —— is Christ's Vicar General, and is the true and only Head of the catholic or universal church throughout the earth; and that by the virtue of the keys of binding and losing, given to his Holiness by my Saviour Jesus Christ, he hath power to depose heretical kings, princes, states, commonwealths, and governments, all being illegal without his sacred confirmation, and that they may safely be destroyed: therefore, to the utmost of my power, I shall, and will defend this doctrine, and his Holiness' rights and customs, against all usurpers of the heretical (or Protestant) authority whatsoever; especially against the now pretended authority and Church of England, and all adherents, in regard that they and she be usurpal and heretical, opposing the sacred mother Church of Rome. I do renounce and disown any allegiance as due to any heretical king, prince, or State, named Protestants, or obedience to any of their inferior magistrates or officers. I do further declare that the doctrine of the Church of England, the Calvinists, Huguenots, and of others of the name Protestants, to be damnable, and they themselves are damned, and to be damned, that will not forsake the same. I do further declare, that I will help, assist and advise all or any of his Holiness' agents in any place wherever I shall be in England, Scotland, and Ireland, or in any other territory or kingdom I shall come to, and do my utmost to extirpate the heretical Protestant's doctrine, and to destroy all their pretended powers, regal or otherwise. I do further promise and declare, that notwithstanding I am dispensed with, to assume any religion heretical, for the propagating of the mother church's interest, to keep secret and private all her agent's counsels, from time to time, as they entrust me, and not to divulge. directly or indirectly, by word, writing, or circumstance whatsoever, but to execute all that shall be proposed, given in charge, or discovered unto me, by you, my ghostly father, or any of this sacred convent. All which, I, A. B., do swear by the blessed Trinity, and blessed Sacrament, which I am now to receive, to perform, and on my part to keep inviolably; and do call all the heavenly and glorious host of heaven to witness these my real intentions, to keep this my oath. In testimony hereof, I take this most holy and blessed Sacrament of the Eucharist; and witness the same further with my hand and seal, in the face of this holy convent, this   day of An. Dom." &c.

OATH OF A LAYMAN,

Commonly called the Creed of Pope Pius IV.

I, N. N., with a firm faith believe and profess all and every one of those things which are contained in that creed which the holy Roman Church maketh use of. To-wit: I believe in one God, the Father Almighty, Maker of heaven and earth, of all things visible and invisible: and in one Lord, Jesus Christ, the only-begotten Son of God, born of the Father before all ages; God of God; Light of light; true God of the true God; begotten, not made, consubstantial with the Father, by whom all things were made. Who for us men, and for our salvation, came down from heaven, and was incarnate by the Holy Ghost of the Virgin Mary, and was made man. He was crucified also for us under Pontius Pilate, suffered, and was buried. And the third day he rose again according to the Scriptures: he ascended into heaven, sitteth at the right hand of the Father, and shall come again with glory to judge the living and the dead; of whose kingdom there shall be no end. I believe in the Holy Ghost, the Lord and the life-giver, who proceedeth from the Father and the Son: who, together with the Father and the Son, is adored and glorified; who spake by the prophets. And in one holy, Catholic and Apostolic Church. I confess one baptism for the remission of sins; and I look for the resurrection of the dead, and the life of the world to come. Amen.

I most steadfastly admit and embrace the apostolical and ecclesiastical Traditions, and all other observances and constitutions of the same Church.

I also admit the holy Scriptures, according to that sense which our holy mother the Church hath held and doth hold, to whom it belongeth to judge of the true sense and interpretation of the Scriptures; neither will I ever take and interpret them otherwise than according to the unanimous consent of the Fathers.

I also profess that there are truly and properly Seven Sacraments of the new law, instituted by Jesus Christ our Lord, and necessary for the salvation of mankind, though not all for every one; to-wit: Baptism, Confirmation, the Eucharist, Penance, Extreme Unction, Order, and Matrimony: and that they confer grace: and that of these, Baptism, confirmation, and Order, cannot be repeated without sacrilege. I also receive and admit the received and approved ceremonies of the Catholic Church, used in the solemn administration of the aforesaid sacraments.

I embrace and receive all and every one of the things which have been defined and declared in the holy Council of Trent concerning original sin and justification.

I profess, likewise, that in the Mass there is offered to God a true, proper and propitiatory sacrifice for the living and the dead. And that in the most holy sacrament of the Eucharist there is truly, really, and substantially the Body and Blood, together with the soul and divinity, of our Lord Jesus Christ; and that there is made a conversion of the whole substance of the bread into the Body, and of the whole substance of the wine into the Blood; which conversion the Catholic Church calleth Transubstantiation. I also confess that under either kind alone Christ is received whole and entire, and a true sacrament.

I constantly hold that there is a Purgatory, and that the souls therein detained are helped by the suffrages of the faithful.

Likewise, that the saints reigning together with Christ are to be honored and invocated, and that they offer prayers to God for us, and that their relics are to be had in veneration.

I most firmly assert that the images of Christ, of the Mother of God ever Virgin, and also of other Saints, ought to be had and retained, and that due honor and veneration are to be given them.

I also affirm that the power of Indulgences was left by Christ in the Church and that the use of them is most wholesome to Christian people.

I acknowledge the Holy, Catholic, Apostolic, Roman Church for the mother and mistress of all Churches; and I promise true obedience to the Bishop of Rome successor of St. Peter, Prince of the Apostles, and Vicar of Jesus Christ.

I likewise undoubtedly receive and profess all other things delivered, defined, and declared by the sacred canons and General Councils, and particularly by the holy Council of Trent. And I condemn, reject and anathematize all things contrary thereto, and all heresies which the Church hath condemned, rejected, and anathematized

I, N. N., do at this present freely profess and sincerely hold this true Catholic faith, out of which no one can be saved: and I promise most constantly to retain and confess the same entire and inviolate, by God's assistance, to the end of my life.

EXTRACTS

Taken from *" The Garden of the Soul,"* touching Extreme Unction, or Anointing with Oil; with the approbation of the Right Rev. Dr. HUGHES, Bishop of New York.

Page 263 (James 5th and 14th), "And as the eyes, the ears, and the other organs of sense, are the instruments by which men are led to offend Almighty God, and they will, on that account, be anointed with holy oil; whilst the priest applies this holy oil to your eyes, your ears, and the REST, "&c., &c., &c., "do you, with a contrite and humble heart, implore the mercy of God for the forgiveness of all the sins which through these respective avenues have made their way into your soul." Taken from the Bank of Pope John 22, A. D. 1316. Those who have defloured a virgin, must pay six gros (seven French sous). "Whoever has carnally known mother, sister, cousin-german, or his god-mother, is taxed one ducat and five carlins" (or five sous).

The Rev. W. Hogan says, in his book on auricular confession, page 49: "That he was acquainted with three priests in Albany, who in less than three years were the fathers of between sixty and one hundred children, besides having debauched many who had left the place previous to their confinement. Many of these children were by married women."

Pages 213 and 214. "VI. Have you been guilty of fornication, or adultery, or incest, or any sin against nature, either with a person of the same sex, or with any other creature? How often? Or have you designed, or attempted any such sin, or sought to induce others to it? How often?

" Have you been guilty of self-pollution? **or** of immodest touches of yourself? How often?

" Have you touched others, or permitted yourself to be touched by others, immodestly? or given or taken wanton kisses or embraces, or any such liberties? How often?

" Have you looked at immodest objects with pleasure or danger? read immodest books or songs to yourselves or others? kept indecent pictures? willingly given ear to, and taken pleasure in hearing, loose discourse, &c.? or sought to see or hear anything that was immodest? How often?

"Have you exposed yourself to wanton company? or played at any indecent play? or frequented masquerades, balls, comedies, &c., with danger to your chastity? How often?

"Have you been guilty of any immodest discourses, wanton stories, jests, or songs, or words of double meaning? How often? and before how many? and were the persons to whom you spoke or sung married or single? For all this you are obliged to confess, by reason of the evil thoughts these things are apt to create in the hearers.

"Have you abused the marriage bed by any actions contrary to the order of nature? or by any pollutions? or been guilty of any irregularity, in order to hinder your having children? How often?

"Have you, without a just cause, refused the marriage debt? and what sin followed from it? How often?

"Have you debauched any person that was innocent before? Have you forced any person, or deluded any one by deceitful promises, &c.? or designed or desired to do so? How often? You are obliged to make satisfaction for the injury you have done.

"Have you taught any one evil that he knew not of before? or carried any one to lewd houses, &c.? How often?

Page 216. "IX. Have you willingly taken pleasure in unchaste thoughts or imaginations? or entertained unchaste desires? Were the objects of your desires maids or married persons, or kinsfolks, or persons consecrated to God? How often?

"Have you taken pleasure in the irregular motions of the flesh? or not endeavored to resist them? How often?

"Have you entertained with pleasure the thoughts of saying or doing anything which it would be a sin to say or do? How often?

"Have you had the desire or design of committing any sin? of what sin? How often?

EXTRACTS FROM
PETER DENS' THEOLOGY.

Auszüge aus Peter Dens Theologie.

DE SIGILLO CONFESSIONIS.

Quid est sigillum confessionis sacramentalis?

R. Est obligatio seu debitum celandi ea, quæ ex sacramentali confessione cognoscuntur.—*Dens, tom. vi, p. 227.*

On the Seal of Confession.	**Über das Beicht-Siegel.**
What is the seal of sacramental confession?	Was ist das Siegel der sacramentalen Beichte?
Ans., It is the obligation or duty of concealing those things which are learned from sacramental confession.—Dens, vol. 6, p. 227.	Antw. Es ist die Verbindlichkeit oder Pflicht, dasjenige zu verhehlen, was man aus der sacramentalen Beichte kennen gelernt hat. Dens, Bd. Seite 227.

An potest dari casus, in quo licet frangere sigillum sacramentale?

R. Non potest dari; quamvis ab eo penderet vita aut salus hominis, aut etiam interitus Reipublicæ; neque summus Pontifex in eo dispensare potest; ut proinde hoc sigilli arcanum magis liget, quam obligatio juramenti, voti, secreti naturalis, etc., idque ex voluntate Dei positiva.

Can a case be given in which it is lawful to break the sacramental seal?	Kann ein Fall gegeben werden, in dem es erlaubt ist, das sacramentale Siegel zu brechen?
A. It cannot; although the life or safety of a man depended thereon, or even the destruction of the commonwealth; nor can the Supreme Pontiff give dispen-	Antw. Es kann keiner gegeben werden; wenn auch von demselben das Leben oder das Lebensglück eines Menschen abhienge, oder auch der Untergang des Staats; noch

sation in this; so that on that account, this secret of the seal is more binding than the obligation of an oath, a vow, a natural secret, etc., and that by the positive will of God.

kann der höchste Oberpriester hierin dispensiren, so daß darum dieses Siegels Geheimniß mehr bindet, als die Verbindlichkeit eines Eides, eines Gelübdes, eines natürlichen Geheimnisses etc., und das nach dem positiven Willen Gottes.

Quid igitur respondere debet Confessarius interrogatus super veritate, quam per solam confessionem sacramentalem novit?

R. Debet respondere se nescire eam, et si opus est, idem juramento confirmare.

What answer then ought a confessor give when questioned concerning a truth which he knows from sacramental confession only?

A. *He ought to answer that he does not know it, and if it be necessary, to confirm the same with an oath.*

Was soll daher der gefragte Beichtvater antworten über die Wahrheit, die er blos durch die sacramentale Beichte weiß?

Antw. Er soll antworten, daß er sie nicht wisse und wenn es nöthig ist, dieses mit einem Eide erhärten.

Obj. Nullo casu licet mentiri; atqui Confessarius ille mentiretur quia scit veritatem, ergo, etc.

R. Neg. min., quia talis Confessarius interrogatur ut homo, et respondet ut homo; jam autem non scit ut homo illam veritatem, quamvis sciat ut Deus, ait S. Th. q. II, art. 1, ad 3, et iste sensus sponte in est responsioni; nam quando extra confessionem interrogatur, vel respondet, consideratur ut homo.

Obj. It is in no case lawful to tell a lie, but that Confessor would be guilty of a lie, because he knows the truth, therefore, etc.

A. I deny the minor; because such a confessor is questioned as a man, and answers as a man; but

Einwendung: 'Es ist in keinem Falle erlaubt zu lügen, nun würde jener Beichtvater aber lügen, weil er die Wahrheit weiß, daher etc.

Antw. Ich verneine den zweiten Satz, weil ein solcher Beichtvater gefragt wird als Mensch, auch er

now he does not know that truth as a man, though he knows it as God, says St. Thomas (q. 11. art. 1, 3), and that is the free and natural meaning of the answer, for when he is asked, or when he answers outside confession, he is considered as a man.

Quid si directe a Confessario quæratur, utrum illud sciat per confessionem sacramentalem?

R. Hoc casu nihil oportet respondere; ita Steyært cum Sylvio; sed interrogatio rejicienda est tanquam impia vel etiam posset absolute, non relative ad petitionem dicere; ego nihil scio; quia vox *ego* restringit ad scientiam humanam.—*Dens, tom. vi, p. 228.*

What if a Confessor were directly asked whether he knows it through sacramental confession?

A. In this case he ought to give no answer (so Steyart and Sylvius), but reject the question as impious: or he could even say absolutely, not relatively to the question. I know nothing, because the word I restricts to his human knowledge.—Dens, v. 6, p. 228.

DE ABSOLUTIONE COMPLICIS.

"Advertendum quod nullus Confessarius, extra mortis periculum, licet alias habeat potestatem absolvendi à reservatis absolvere possit aut valeat à peccato quolibet mortali externo contra castitatem, complicem in eodem secum peccato."

Hic casus complicis non collocatur inter casus reservatos, quia Episcopus non reservat sibi absolutionem, sed quilibet alius Confessarius potest ab eo absolvere, præterquam sacerdos complex. *Ib. 6, 297.*

On the Absolution of an Accomplice.

"Let it be observed that, except in case of danger of death, no Confessor, though he may otherwise have the power of absolving from reserved cases, may or can absolve his accomplice in any external mortal sin against chastity committed by the accomplice with the Confessor himself."

This case of an accomplice is NOT *placed amongst the reserved cases, because the Bishop does* NOT *reserve the absolution to himself, but any other Confessor can absolve from it, except the priest who is himself the partner in the act.*

Abſolution eines Mitſchuldigen.

"Es iſt zu beachten, daß kein Beichtvater, außer in der Gefahr des Todes, obwohl er ſonſt die Macht haben mag, in vorbehaltenen Fällen zu abſolviren — abſolviren kann oder vermag von irgend einer tödlichen äußeren Sünde gegen die Keuſchheit, eine Perſon, die mit ihm gemeinſchaftlich ſolche Sünde begangen hat."

Dieſer Fall eines Mitſchuldigen iſt nicht unter die vorbehaltenen Fälle zu ſetzen, weil der Biſchof ſich die Abſolution nicht vorbehält, ſondern irgend ein anderer Beichtvater kann davon abſolviren außer der mitſchuldig Prieſter.

An comprehenditur masculus complex in peccato venereo v. g. per tactus?

R. Affirmative, quia Pontifex extendit ad qualemcumque personam.

Non requiritur ut hoc peccatum complicis patratum sit in confessione, vel occasione confessionis; quocumque enim loco vel tempore factum est, etiam antequam esset Confessarius, facit casum complicis. *Ib. 6, 298.*

Is a male accomplice in venereal sin, to wit, by touches, comprehended in this degree?

A. Yes, because the Pope extends it to whatsoever person.

It is not required that this sin of an accomplice be committed in confession, or by occasion of confession; for in whatever place or

Wird eine männliche Perſon als Mitſchuldiger an der fleiſchlichen Sünde angeſehen, z. B. durch Taſten?

Antw. Ja, weil der Pontifer (Pabſt) es auf jede Perſon ausdehnt.

Es wird nicht erfordert, daß dieſe Sünde des Mitſchuldigen während

time it has been done, even before he was her confessor, it makes a case of an accomplice

der Beichte begangen word n sei, oder gelegenheitlich der Beichte; denn an was immer für einem Orte oder zu welcher Zeit es auch geschah, auch selbst wenn vorher ehe er noch Beichtvater war, der Fall der Mitschuldnerschaft ist vorhanden.

Nota ultimo, cum restrictio fiat ad peccata carnis, poterit Confessarius complicem in aliis peccatis, v. g. in furto, homocidio, etc., valide absolvere.—*Dens, tom. vi, 298.*

Lastly, take note, that since the restriction is made to carnal sins, the Confessor will be able to give valid absolution to his accomplice in other sins, namely, in theft, in homicide, etc.—Dens, v. 6, pp. 297–8.

Endlich beichte man, daß, da die Einschränkung auf Fleischessünden gemacht ist, der Beichtvater den Mitschuldigen von andern Sünden, z. B. Diebstahl, Mord etc. giltig absolviren kann. Dens, Bd. 6. S. 298.

After telling us, that in obedience to a bull of Gregory the Fifteenth, and a constitution founded thereon by Benedict the Fourteenth, any Priest is to be denounced who endeavors to seduce his penitents in the Confessional, he asks the following question:

Der Verfasser bemärkt hier, daß gemäß einer Bulle Gregor's 15. und einer von Benedict 14. darauf gegründeten Constitution, jeder Priester benunzirt werden soll, der seine Beichtkinder im Beichtstuhl zu verfüren sucht, und stellt sobann die folgende Frage:

Confessarius sollicitavit pœnitentem ad turpia, non in confessione, nec occasione confessionis, sed ex alia occasione extraordinariâ: an est denuntiandus?

R. Negative. Aliud foret, si ex scientiâ confessionis sollicitaret; quia, v. g., ex confessione novit; illam personam deditam tali peccato venereo.—*P. Antoine, t. iv, p. 430.*

A Confessor has seduced his penitent to the commission of carnal sin, not in confession, nor by occasion of confession, but from some other extraordinary occasion: Is he to be denounced?

A. No. If he had tampered with her from his knowledge of

Ein Beichtvater hat sein Beichtkind zur Fleischessünde verführt, nicht während die Beichte, auch nicht gelegenheitlich des Beichthörens, sonder bei einer ganz andern Gelegenheit: soll man ihn denunziren?

Antw. Nein. Ein anderer Fall wäre es, wenn er sie in Folge des-

confession, it would be a different tl.ing, because, for instance, he knows that person, from her confession, to be given to such carnal sins. P. Antoine, t. 4, p. 430.

fen, was er im Beichtstuhl erfahren hat, verführt hätte, z. B. weil er wußte, daß sie eine Person sei, die solchen Fleischessünden ergeben ist. P. Antoine, B. 4. S. 430.

Propterea monet Steyærtius, quod Confessarius pœnitentem, qui confitctur se peccasse cum Sacerdote, vel sollicitatum ab eo ad turpia. interrogare possit utrum ille sacerdos sit ejus Confessarius, an in Confessione sollicitaverit, etc.

For which reason Steyart reminds us that a Confessor can ask a penitent, who confesses that she has sinned with a priest, or has been seduced by him to the commission of carnal sin, whether that priest was her Confessor or had seduced her in the Confessional.

Deßhalb erinnert Steyert daran, daß der Beichtvater das Beichtkind, welches bekennt, mit einem Priester gesündigt zu haben, oder von ihm zu Fleischessünde verführt worden zu sein, fragen könne, ob jener Priester ihr Beichtvater sei, und ob er sie in der Beichte verführt habe, etc

An denuntiatio fieri debet, quando dubium est, utrum fuerit vera et sufficiens sollicitatio ad turpia?

R. Quidam negant, sed Card. Cozza cum aliis, quos citat, dub. 25, affirmat, si dubium non sit leve, dicens examen illud relinqvendum Episcopo sive Ordinario.—*Dens, t. vi, p. 301.*

Ought the denunciation be made when there exists a doubt whether the soliciation to carnal sin was real and sufficient?
A. Some say No, but Card. Cozza, with others whom he cites, doubt 25, says yes, if the doubt be not light, adding that the examidation of the matter is to be left to the Bishop or the ordinary. —Dens, v. 6, p. 301.

Or eine Denunziation geschehen soll wenn zweifelhaft ist, ob es eine wirkliche und hinreichende Verführung zur Fleischessünde war?
Antw. Manche verneinen das, aber Card. Cozza mit andern, die er anführt, 25. Zweifel, bejaht es; wenn der Zweifel nicht unbedeutend, so sagt er, daß die Untersuchung dem Bischoff oder dem Ordinarius überlassen werden soll. Dens Bd. 6. S. 301.

DE MODO DENUNTIANDI SOLLICITANTEM PRÆFATUM.

Primus modus magis conveniens est. si ipsa persona sol-
licitata immediate,nulli,alteri revelando, accedat Episcopum
sive Ordinarium. 2o, Potest Episcopo scribere epistolam
clausam et signatam sub hac formâ: "Ego Catharina N.,
habitans Mechlinæ in plateâ N. sub signo N. hisce declaro
me 6 Martii anno 1758 occasione confessionis fuisse sollicitatum ad inhonesta a Confessario N. N. excipiente confessiones Mechlinæ, in Ecclesiâ N. quod juramento confirmare
parata sum."—*Dens, tom. vi, 302.*

On the Mode of Denouncing the aforesaid Seducer.	über die Art, wie der vorerwähnte Verführer zu denunziren sei.
The first and most convenient mode is this, if the person upon whose chastity the attempt had been made, would proceed herself immediately to the Bishop or the Ordinary, without revealing the circumstance to any one else. 2d. She can write a letter closed and sealed to the Bishop in the following form: "I, Catharine N., dwelling at Mechlin, in the street N., under the sign N., by these declare that I, on the 6th day of March, 1758, on the occasion of confession, have been seduced to improper acts by the Confessor N., hearing confessions at Mech- lin, in the church N., which I am ready to confirm on oath.	Die erste und passendste Art ist, wenn die verführte Person selbst unmittelbar, ohne irgend jemand sonst etwas davon zu offenbaren zum Bischof oder Ordinarius geht. 2tens. Sie kann dem Bischof in einem verschlossenen und versiegelten Briefe schr... n, nach dieser Form: "Ich Katharina N., von wohnhaft zu Mecheln in Straße N., unter dem Schilde N., erkläre hiermit, daß ich am 6 März 1758 bei Gele- genheit der Beichte zu unehrbaren Dingen verführt worden bin durch den Beichtvater N. N., der Beichte hört in der N. Kirche zu Mecheln, was ich durch meinen Eid zu bekräf- tigen bereit bin."

3d. Si autem scribere nequeat, similis epistola scribatur
ab alio v. g. à secundo Confessario cum licentià pœnitentis. et nomen pœnitentis, et nomen pœnitentis seu personæ
sollicitantis, exprimatur ut suprà: sed nomen Confessarii
sollicitantis ut occultum maneat scribenti, non expri-

matur, verùm à tertio aliquo, rei ignaro, in chartulà aliqua nomen ejus scribatur sub alio prætexta; quæ chartula epistolæ præfatæ includatur.

3d. But if she cannot write, let a similar letter be written by another, namely, by a second Confessor, with the license of the penitent, and let the name of the penitent or person seduced be expressed as above, but let the name of the seducing confessor, in order that it may remain a secret to the writer, be not expressed, but let his name be written under a different pretext, by some third person ignorant of the circumstances, on some scrap of paper which may be enclosed in the aforesaid letter.

3tens. Wenn sie aber nicht schreiben kann, so soll ein ähnlicher Brief von einem andern geschrieben werden, z. B. vom zweiten Beichtvater, mit Einwilligung des Beichtkindes und der Name des Beichtkindes oder der verführten Person soll ausgedrückt werden, wie oben; aber der Name des verführenden Priesters, damit er dem Schreiber des Briefes verborgen bleibe, soll nicht ausgedrückt werden, sondern von irgend einem der nichts weiß, von der Sache, soll der Name desselben auf einen Zettel geschrieben werden, unter einem andern Vorwande, welcher Zettel dann dem vorbesagten Briefe anzuschließen ist.

In hoc casu (denunciationis) tamen quidam putant moderandum, et considerandas esse circumstantias frequentiæ, periculi, etc.—*Dens, tom. vi. p. 301.*

In this case (of denouncing), however, some are of opinion that moderation must be observed, and that the circumstances of frequency, of danger, etc., must be considered.—Dens, vol. 6, p. 301.

Iag In Falle (der Denunziation, esemuben jedoch einige, daß man mit Mäßigung verfahren müsse, und die Umstände des Frequenz, der Gefahr etc. zu erwägen seien.— Dens, Bd. 6. S. 301.

Monentur interea Confessarii, ut mulierculis quibuscumque accusantibus priorem Confessarium, fidem leviter non adhibeant; sed prius scrutentur accusationis finem et causam, examinent earum mores, conversatiónem, etc. — *Ib. vi. 302.*

In the mean time, Confessors are advised not lightly to give

Inzwischen werden die Beichtväter angewiesen, dergleichen Frau-

credit to any woman whatsoever accusing their former Confessor, but first to search diligently into the end and cause of the occasion, to examine their morals, conversation, etc.

enzimmerchen, die ihren vorigen Beichtvater anklagen, nicht so leicht Glauben zu schenken, sondern vorher das Ende und die Ursache der Gelegenheit zu durchforschen, ihre Sitten, Conversation zu prüfen, etc.

Quocirca observa, quod quæcumque persona, quæ per se vel per aliam, falsò denuntiat sacerdotem tanquàm sollicitatorem, incurrat casum reservatum summo Potifici. Ita Benedictus XIV. Constit. Sacramentum Pœnitent. apud Antoine, p. 418.

For which reason observe, that whatever person, either by herself or by another, falsely denounces a priest as a seducer, incurs a case reserved for the supreme Pontiff. Thus Benedict the Fourteenth, in the constitution, called "Sacramentum Pœnitentiæ," in Antoine, p. 418.

Daher beachte man, daß, welche Person immer, die selbst oder durch eine andere einen Priester als Verführer falsch anklagt, sich einem dem höchsten Oberpriester (Pabst) vorbehaltenen Falle aussetzt. So Benedict XIV, Constit. Sacrament der Beichte bei, Antoine, S. 418.

Benedictus XIV. in Constit. citata numero 216, reservavit sibi et successoribus peccatum falsæ denuntiationis Confessarii sollicitantis ad turpia.—*Dens, tom. vi. p. 303.*

Benedict the Fourteenth, in the Constitution cited in No. 216, reserves to himself and his successors the sin of falsely denouncing a Confessor for seducing his penitent to commit carnal sin.—Dens, vol. 6. p. 303.

Benedict der XIV in der angeführten Constitution, behält sich und seinen Nachfolgern unter No. 216 der Fall der falschen Anklage eines Priesters als Verführer zur Fleischessünde, vor. — Dens, Bd. 6. S. 803.

Alloquium puellæ est occasio proxima illi qui ex decem vicibus bis vel ter solet cadere in peccatum carnis vel in delectationem carnis deliberatam. — *Ib. vi. 185.*

Speaking to a girl is a proximate occasion (of sin) to him,

Das Reden mit einem Mädchen ist solche Annäherungsgelegenheit,

who, out of every ten times, is wont to fall twice or thrice into carnal sin, or into deliberate carnal delight.

welche in zehn Fällen zwei oder dreimal in Fleischessünde oder vorbedachte Fleischeslust auszufallen pflegt.

Frequentatio quotidiana tabernæ aut puellæ censetur esse occasio proxima respectu ejus, qui ex ea bis vel ter inmense prolabitur in simile peccatum mortale.— *Vol. vi. p. 185.*

Daily frequenting a tavern or a girl is considered a proximate occasion (of sin) in respect of him, who, on that account, falls twice or thrice a month into like mortal sin.—Vol. vi., p. 185.

Der tägliche Besuch eines Wirthshauses oder eines Mädchens wird in Beziehung auf ihn als eine Annäherungs = Gelegenheit betrachtet, und er fällt deshalb zwei oder dreimal im Monat in ähnliche Todsünde.

Idem resolvit P. Du Jardin, p. 51, de administratione quotidiana alicujus officii licet honesti, v. g. Medici, Confessarii, Causidici, Mercatoris, si inde quis bis terve per mensem deliberate cadere soleat, et pag. 53 concludit Confessarium obligari ad deserendum illud ministerium. — *Ib. vi. 185.*

P. Du Jardin is of the same opinion (p. 51) respecting the daily administration of any office, however honest, for instance, of a Physician, a Confessor. a Lawyer, a Merchant, if any should on that account be accustomed to fall deliberately two or three times a month, and in page 53 he concludes that the Confessor is bound to desert that ministry.—Vol. vi., p. 185.

Dasselbe erklärt P. Du Jardin, S. 51, über die Leistung täglicher Dienste, wie ehrbar diese auch seien, z. B. die eines Arztes, eines Beichtvaters, Rechtsanwaltes, Kaufmanns, wenn deßhalb irgend jemand zwei oder dreimal im Monat mit Vorbedacht zu fallen pflegt, und S. 53 kommt er zu dem Schluß, daß ein Beichtvater verbunden ist, ein solches Geschäft zu verlassen.

Obj. Confessarius ille quotidie occupatus in ministerio audiendi confessiones rarissime cadit comparative ad vices, quibus non cadit; ergo ministerium audiendi confessiones respectu illius non est occasio proxima.

Nego cons. quia ille, licet, non comparative, absolute tamen frequenter cadit; qui enim per singulos menses committeret duo vel tria injusta homiocida, diceretur absolute frequenter committere homiocidium, ille Confessarius toties occidit animam suam ergo.—*Dens, tom. 6 p. 185.*

Obj. That Confessror every day occupied in the ministry of hearing confessions, falls very seldom in comparison with the times he does not fall: therefore the ministry of hearing confessions is not with respect to him a proximate occasion (of sin).

A. I deny the consequence, because he, though not comparatively, does, however, absolutely fall frequently, for he who would commit two or three unjust homicides every month, should be said absolutely to commit homicide frequently, so often does that Confessor slay his own soul.— Dens, v. vi., p. 185.

Einwendung: Der täglich mit der Verrichtung des Beichthörens beschäftigte Beichtvater fällt sehr selten in Vergleichung mit der Zeitdauer, in de er nicht fällt, daher die Verrichtung des Beichthörens führ ihn keine Annäherungsgelegenheit ist.

Antw. Ich vernehme den Schluß, weil er, obwohl vergleichungsweise nicht, aber in der That häufig fällt; derjenige nämlich, der jeden Monat zwei oder drei ungerechte Tödtungen begehen wurde, von dem müßte man sagen, daß er in der That häufig Todtschlag begeht; jener Beichtvater tödtet seine eigene Seele.— Dens Bd. 6. S. 185.

De justis causis permittendi Motus Sensualitatis.

JUSTA CAUSA EST AUDITIO CONFESSIONUM.

Quanta debet esse causa, ob quam quis se possit habere permissive ad motus inordinatus, sic ut illi motus non censeantur voluntarii nec culpabiles?

R. Debet esse tanta ut cum suo effectu bono in his circumstantiis prævaleat istis motibus seu effectui malo, juxta regulam N. 15 explicatam.—*Vol. 1. p. 315.*

On just causes for permitting Motions of Sensuality.

HEARING OF CONFESSION IS JUST CAUSE.

How great ought to be the cause for which one can hold himself permissively with regard to

Über die rechtmäßigen Ursachen, Erregungen der Sinnlichkeit zuzulassen.

Das Beichthören ist eine rechtmäßige Ursache.

26 DENS' THEOLOGY.

inordinate motions, so as that they may be considered neither voluntary nor culpable?

A. It ought to be so great as to prevail with its good effect in these circumstances, over those motions or the bad effect, according to the rule explained in No. 15.—Vol. i., p. 315

Wie groß muß die Ursache sein, aus der jemand für sich unordentliche Gemüthsbewegungen zuläßig ansehen kann, so, daß seine Erregungen weber als aus eigenem Willen entstonden, noch als strafbar zu errachten sind?

Antw. Dieselbe muß so groß sein, daß sie mit ihrer guten Wirkung bei diesen Umständen die Erregungen oder die schlechte Wirkung überwiegt, nach der Regel, die No. 15 erklärt ist.

Hujusmodi justæ causæ sunt auditio confessionum, lectio casuum conscientiæ pro Confessario, servitium necessarium vel utile Præstitum infirmo.— *Vol. i. p. 315.*

Just causes of this sort are the hearing of confessions, the reading of cases of conscience drawn up for a Confessor, necessary or useful attendance on an invalid. — Vol. i., p. 315.

Gerechte Ursachen der Art sind Beichthören, das Lesen von Abhandlungen über Gewissensfälle für Beichtväter, nothwendige oder nützliche Dienstleistungen bei einem Gebrechlichen.

Justa causa facere potest, ut opus aliquod, ex quo motus oriuntur, non tantum licite inchoetur, sed etiam licite continuetur: et ita Confessarius ex auditione Confessionis eos percipiens, non ideo ab auditione abstinere, debet, sed justam habet perseverandi rationem, modo tamen ipsi motus illi semper displiceant, nec inde oriatur proximum periculum consensus.—*Dens, tom. 1. p. 315.*

The effect of a just cause is such, that anything from which motions arise, may be not only lawfully begun, but also lawfully continued, and so the Confessor receiving those motions from the hearing of confessions, ought not

Die gerechte Ursache kann machen, daß solche Beschäftigungen, aus denen die Erregungen entstehen, nicht blos erlaubterweise begonnen, sondern auch erlaubterweise fortgesetzt werden, un so der Beichtvater, dem dieselben beim Beichthören

on that account to abstain from hearing them, but has a just cause for persevering, providing, however, that they always displease him, and there arise not therefrom the proximate danger of consent. —Dens, v. i., p. 315.

wiederfahren, deßhalb vom Beicht= hören nicht abzugehen verbünden ist, sondern gerechten Grund zum Fort= fahren hat; jedoch so, daß jene Er= regungen ihm stets mißfällig sind, und daraus nicht die nahe Gefahr der Zustimmung entstehe. — Dens, Bd. 1 S. 315.

In omni peccato carnali circumstantia conjugii sit exprimenda in confessione.— *Vol. vii. p. 167.*

In every carnal sin, let the circumstance of marriage be expressed in confession.

Es soll bei dem Beichten jeder Fleischessünde der Umstand der Ver= ehelichtung angegeben werden.

An aliquando interrogandi sunt conjugati in confessione circa negationem debiti?

R. Affirmative præsertim mulieres, quæ ex ignorantia vel præ pudore peccatum istud quandoque reticent: verum non ex abrupto, sed prudenter est interrogatio instituenda v. g. an cum marito rixatæ sint, quæ hujusmodi rixarum causa; num propter talem occasionem maritis debitum negarint; quod si se deliquisse fateantur, caste interrogari debent, an nil secutum fuerit continentiæ conjugali contrarium, v. g. pollutio, &c.— *Vol. vii. p. 167.*

Are the married to be at any time asked in confession about denying the marriage duty?

A. YES: particularly the WOMEN* who, through igno-

Sollen Eheleute jemals bei der Beichte wegen Verweigerung der ehelichen Pflicht befragt werden?

Antw. Allerdings: insbesondere die Weiber,*) die aus Unwissenheit

---

*WOMEN—The following passage is taken from the Moral Theology, in which the young priests are lectured in Maynooth : the reader will perceive that it is almost word for word the same as that selected from Peter Dens :

*) Weiber. — Folgende Stelle ist der moralischen Theologie entnommen, über welche die jungen Priester in Maynooth Vorlesungen erhalten. Der Leser wird be= cherfen, daß dieselbe fast Wort für Wort das Nämliche ist, was hier aus Peter Dens gewählt wurde:

rance or modesty, are sometimes
silent on that sin ; but the question is not to be put abruptly, but
to be framed prudently, for instance, whether they have quar-
reled with their husbands ; what
was the cause of these quarrels :

oder Schamhaftigkeit zuweilen diese
Sunde verschweigen ; aber nicht un=
erwartet plötzlich ist die Frage zu
stellen, sondern mit Vorsicht, z. B.
ob sie sich mit dem manne zanken ;
was die Ursache dieses Streits ist,
ob siie dem Manne bei solchen Ge=

QUÆRES 1o. An teneantur conjuges reddere debitum ?

R. Tenere utramque conjugem sub mortali injustitiæ peccato
comparti reddere debitum, dum vel expresse vel tacite exigitur, nisi
legitima causa de negandi intervenerit. Id constat ex S. Paulo. 1
Corinth. vii.

Dixi autem 1o. UTRUMQUE CONJUGEM TENERI ; in eo enim pares sunt
ambo conjuges, ut patet ex verbis Apostoli.

Dixi 2o, eos teneri SUB PECCATO MORTALI, quia res est per se gravis,
cum inde nascantur rixæ odia dissensiones parsaque debito fraudata
incontinentiæ periculo exponatur : quod lethale est. Hinc Parochus
aut per se in Tribunali Pœnitentiæ ant saltem, et quidem aliquando
prudentius piæ matris ministerio, adocere debet sponsas, quid in hac
parte observandum sit. Cum vero mulieres ejusmodi peccata in confessione sacramentali præ pudore aut ignorantia non raro reticeant ex-
pedit aliquando de iis illas interrogare, sed caute et prudentur, non
ex abrupto : v. g. inquiri potest an disidia fuerint inter eam et conjugem, quæ eorum causæ, qui effectus. an propterea marito denegav-
erit quod ex conjugii legibus ei debetur.—[Maynooth Class Book,
Tract de Matrimo p. 482.

Are man and wife bound to render
each other matrimonial duty ?

A. Each is bound under a mortal sin
of injustice to render matrimonial duty
to his or her partner, whilst it is ex-
pressly or tactily required, unless there
should occur a legitimate reason for re-
fusing. That is manifest from St. Paul.
1 Corinth, Chap. vii

But I have said that each is bound,
for in this affair both man and wife are
equal, as is clear from the words of the
Apostle.

sind, siich gegenseitig die eheliche Pflichte
zu leisten?

Antw. Jeder der ehegotten ist bei Ver=
meidung der Todsünde der Ungerechtigkeit,
verbunden, seinem gatten die eheliche
Pflicht zu leisten, indem es entweder aus=
brücklich oder stillschweigend erfordert wird
wenn nicht eine rechtmäßige Ursache der
Verweigerung eintritt. Dieseg ergibt sich
aus St. Paulus 1. Kor. 7.

Ich habe aber 1tens gesagt, daß j e b e r
e h e g a t t e b a z u v e r b u n d e n
ist, denn hierin sind beide Ehegatten

whether they did upon these occasions deny their husbands the marriage duty; but if they acknowledge they have transgressed, they ought to be asked chastely, WHETHER ANYTHING FOLLOWED CONTRARY TO CONJUGAL CONTINENCE, viz., POLLUTION,* etc.

legenheiten ⸗le eheliche Pflichte verweigern; wenn sie nun bekennen, daß sie sich dieses zu Schulden kommen ließen, so sind sie züchtig zu fragen, ob irgend etwas alsdann vorgefallen, was gegen die eheliche Enthaltsamkeit ist, z. B. Pollution, etc.*)

I have said in the second place, that they are bound under MORTAL SIN, because it is a weighty affair in itself, since it is the active cause of quarrels, hates, dissensions, and since the party defrauded of duty is exposed to the danger of incontinence, which is a deadly sin: hence the Parish Priest, either himself personally in the Tribunal of Penance (the Confessional), or at least (and sometimes more prudently) by the agency of a pious matron, ought to inform married persons, and PARTICULARLY MARRIED WOMEN, of what they should observe with respect to this matter. But since women, through modesty or ignorance, not unfrequently conceal sins of that sort in sacramental confession, it is expedient sometimes to interrogate them regarding those sins, but cautiously, prudently, not abruptly; for instance, it may be asked whether there have been any dissensions between her and her husband; what was the cause—and what the effect of them—whether she has on that account denied to her husband what is due to him by the laws of marriage.—Maynooth Class Book, Tract on Matrimony, p. 482.

1ste Frage. Ob die Eheleute verbunden gleichberechtigt, wie aus den Worten des Apostels erhellt.

2tens habe ich gesagt, daß sie bei Todsünde dazu verbunden sind, da es eine an sich wichtige Sache ist, indem hieraus Zwistigkeiten, Gehässigkeiten, Uneinigkeiten entstehen, und der um die Pflicht betrogene Theil der Gefahr der Unenthaltsamkeit ausgesetzt wird, was tödliche Sünde ist. Daher sollte der Ortspriester entweder, wie sich von selbst versteht, in dem Tribunal der Buße (Beichtstuhl), oder wenigstens, was manchmal klüger ist, durch Vermittlung einer frommen Frauensperson, die Eheleute darüber belehren lassen, was in der Sache zu thun ist. Da aber Weiber derartige Sünden in der sacramentalen Beichte nicht selten aus Schamhaftigkeit oder Unwissenheit verschweigen, so ist es oft angemessen sie zu fragen, jedoch vorsichtig un klüglich, nicht unerwartet plötzlich, z. B. man kann fragen, ob zwischen ihr und dem Manne Uneingkeiten vorgefallen sind, was die Ursache derselben ist, was der Erfolg; ob sie deshalb dem Manne verweigert habe, was iom nach den Ehegesetzen gebührt. — (Maynooth ClassBuch, Abhandlung De Matrim., S. 482.)

Notatur, quod pollutio in mulieribus quandoque possit perfici, ita ut semen earum non effluat extra membrum genitale; indicium istius allegat Billuart, si scilicet mulier sentiat seminis resolutionem cum magno voluptatis sensu, qua completa passio satiatur.—Dens, tom. 4 p. 363.

*It is remarked that women may be guilty of perfect pollution, even without

*) Es wird bemerkt, daß zuweilen be Weibern die Pollution vollendet sein kann,

Hinc uxor se accusans in confessione quod negaverit debitum interrogetur, an maritus ex pleno rigore juris sui id
petiverit; idque colligetur, ex eo, quod petiverit instanter,
quod graviter fuerit offensus, quod aversiones vel alia mala
sint secuta, de quibus etiam se accusare debet, nuia fuit
eorum causa; contra si confiteatur rixas vel aversiones ad-
versus maritum interrogari potest; an debitum negaverit?
Dens, vii. p. 168.

Hence let the wife accusing herself in confession of having denied the marriage duty, be asked whether the husband demanded it with the full rigor of his right; and that shall be inferred from his having demanded it instantly, from his having been grievously offended, or from aversions or any other evils having followed of which she ought also to accuse herself, because she was the cause of them; on the other hand, if she confess that there exist quarrels and aversions between her and her husband, she can be asked, whether she has denied the marriage duty.—Dens, v. vii., *p. 168.*

Hiernach frage man die der Ver- weigerung der eheliche Pflicht sich anflagende Frau, ob der Mann die- selbe nach der ganzen Strenge fei- nes Rechtes verlangt habe; dieses soll daraus erkannt werden, wenn er sich unverzüglich verlangt hat; wenn er empfindlich beleidigt war und wenn Wiederwärtigkeiten oder andere Übel erfolgt sind, deren sich die Frau, weil sie die Ursache der- selben war, anflagen sollte; da- gegen, wenn sie beichtet, daß Zän- fereien und Mißhelligfeiten zwischen ihr und dem Manne bestehen, so kann sie gefragt werden, ob sie die eheliche Pflicht verweigert habe.— Dens, Bd. 7. S. 168.

Variis modis peccari potest contra bonum prolis, scilicet*

a flow of their semen to the outside of the genital member (the passage); of which Billuart alleges a proof, if, for in- stance, the women feel a resolution (loosening) of the semen with a great sense of pleasure, which being com- pleted, HER PASSION IS SATIATED.—Dens, v. iv., p. 380.

auch wenn ihr fame nicht aus dem Ge- schlechtstheil fließt. Billuart giebet hiervon ein Kennzeichen an, nämlich wenn das Weib das Abgehen des Samens mit gro- fein Wohllustgefühl empfindet, wobei sie vollen Affect fühlt. – Dens, Bd. 4. S. 380.

*Quid est bonum prolis?

R. Legitima prolis generatio et ejusdem inveni Dei cultu educa
cio.—*Dens, t. 7 p. 164.*

1o. peccant viri, qui committut peccatum Her et Onan quos, qu'a rem hanc detestatem fecerunt, interfecit Dominus. Genesis 38.

Sin can in various modes be committed against the good of the offspring: 1stly, the men sin who commit the sin of Her and Onan, whom, because they did this detestable thing the Lord slew. Genesis xxxviii.

Es kann gegen das Gute der Nachkommenschaft auf verschiedene Art gesündigt werden, nämlich*)

1., die Männer sündigen, welche die Sünde des Ger und Onan begehen, die, weil sie diese abscheuungswürdige Sünde begiengen, der Herr getödtet hat.—1. Mos. c. 38.

2. Pecant uxores, quæ potionibus fœtus conceptionem impediunt, aut susceptum viri semen ejiciunt, vel ejicere conantur.—*Dens, tom. 7 p. 165.*

2dly. The wives sin, who prevent the conception of the fœtus with potions, or eject or endeavor to eject the seed received from the man.—Dens, v. vii., p. 165.

2., Die Weiber sündigen, welche durch Tränke die Empfängniß des Fötus hindern, oder den empfangenen männlichen Samen ausschütten, oder zu ausschütten sich bemühen.— Dens, B. 7. S. 165.

Notent hic Confessarii, quod conjugati, ne proles nimium multiplicentur, aliquando committant detestabilem turpitudinem, in similitudinem Her et Onan, circa quod peccatum examinandi sunt.—*Dens, tom. 7 p. 172.*

Here let the Confessor take note. that the married, lest their children multiply too fast, sometimes commit a detestable turpitude like that of Her and Onan, about which sin THEY ARE TO BE EXAMINED.—Dens, v. vii., p. 172.

Die Beichtväter sollen hierbei darauf achten, daß Eheleute nicht, damit ihre Kinderzahl nicht zu stark werde, manchmal eine verabscheuungswürdige Sünde begehen, ähnlich der des Ger und Onan, über welches sie zu befragen sind.— Dens, Bd. 7. S. 172.

---

* What does the good of the offspring mean?

A. It means the legitimate generation of offspring, and the education of the same in the worship of the true God.— Dens, v. vii., p. 146.

*) Was ist das Gute der Nachkommenschaft?

Antw. Die gesetzmäßige Erzeugung von Nachkommen und die Erziehung derselben in wahren Gottesdienst.— Dens, Bd. 7. S. 164.

Ne Confessarius hæreat iners in circumstantiis alicujus peccati indagandis, in promptu habeat hunc circumstantiarum vesiculum :

Lest the Confessor should indolently hesitate in tracing out the circumstances of any sin, let him have the following versicle of circumstances in readiness :—

Damit nicht ein Beichtvater es nachläſſigerweiſe unterlaſſe, die Umſtände irgend einer Sünde auszuforſchen, ſoll er folgende Formel der Erforſchung der Umſtände ſtets bereit haben:

Quis, quid, ubi, quibus, auxiliis, cur, quomodo, quando.—Dens, tom. 6. p. 123

Who, which, where, with, why, how, when?—Dens, v. 6. p. 123.

Wer, was, wo, womit, warum, wie, wann?—Dens, Bd. 6. S. 132.

An Confessarius potest absolvere sponsam dum cognoscit ex solo confessione sponsi, quon sponsa in confessione reticeat fornicationem habitam cum sponso ?

R. Varsas reperio opiniones ; La Croix, lib. 6. p. n. 1969, existimat sponsam non esse absolvendam, sed dissimulanter dicendum ; Miseriatur tui, &c., ita ut ipsa ignoret sibi absolutionem negari.

Can a Confessor absolve a young woman going to be married, whilst he knows solely from the confession of the betrothed husband that she does not disclose in her confession the fornication she has been guilty of with her betrothed ? A. I find various opinions : La Croix thinks that she ought not to be absolved, but that the Confessor should dissemble, and say Miseriatur, tui, &c., so that she may not know that absolution has been denied her.

Kann ein Beichtvater eine Braut abſolviren, wenn er blos aus der Beichte des Bräutigams weiß, daß die Braut die Hurerei, die ſie mit dem Bräutigam zu begehen gewohnt war, in der Beichte verſchwiegen hat? Antwort: Ich fand verſchiedene Meinungen: La Croix, B. 6. S. 1969, meint, daß die Braut nicht zu abſolviren ſei, ſondern zu ihr verſtelterweiſe geſagt werden ſolle: Miseriatur, tui &c., ſo, daß ſie es ſelbſt nicht weiß, daß ihr die Abſolution verweigert wurde.

Prudentes Confessarii solent et statuunt regulariter inquirere ab omnibus sponsis, utrum occasione futuri matrimonii occurrerint cogitationes quaedam inhonesta? Utrum permiserint oscula, et alias majores libertates ad, invicem ex eo, quod forte putaverint jam sibi plura licere?

Prudent Confessors are wont and lay it down regularly to ask from all young women going to be married, whether from occasion of their approaching marriage there occurred to them any improper thoughts? whether they permitted kisses and other greater alternate liberties, because perhaps they thought that greater freedoms would soon be allowed them?

Die klugen Beichväter haben die Gewohnheit und als Grundsatz festgestellt, regelmäßig alle Brautleute zu fragen, ob bei Gelegenheit ihrer künftigen Verehelichung unehrbare Gedanken bei ihnen entstanden sind? Ob sie Küsse und andere größere Freiheiten gegenseitig zuließen, weil sie etwa glaubten, daß ihnen schon mehr erlaubt sei?

Cum verecundia soleat magis corripere sponsam, propterea solemus prius in confessione audire sponsum. ut sponsa postea confidentius exponat, quod novit jam esse notum Confessario.

And since the young woman is more under the influence of modesty, we are wont for that reason to hear the betrothed husband's confession first, that she may afterwards more confidently reveal to the Confessor what she knows to be now known to him.

Da sich Blödigkeit mehr der Braut sich zu bemächtigen pflegt, so haben wir die Gewohnheit, den Bräutigam zuerst beichten zu lassen, damit die Braut nachher zuversichtlicher angebe, wovon sie weiß, daß es dem Beichtvater schon bekannt ist.

Addunt aliqui, sponsum qui prius confitetur, posse, induci; ut dicat sponsae, se peccatum illud aperte esse confessum. Post confessionem sponsae id non licet amplius.—*Dens, tom. 6. pp. 239–40.*

Some Divines add that the betrothed husband, who makes his confession first, can be induced to

Einige fügen bei, daß der Bräutigam, der zuerst beichtet, veranlaßt werden könne, daß er der Braut

3

tell her that he has openly con- fessed that sin. After the young woman's confession that would be no longer in the Confessor's power. —Dens, v, 6. pp. 244.

fage, er habe jene Sünde frei be kannt. Nach der Beichte der Braut würde daß nicht mehr statthaft fein.—Dens, Bd. 6. S. 244

An licita est delectatio morosa de opere jure naturae prohibitio, sed sine culpa formali hic et nunc posito, v. g. delectatio de pollutione nocturno involuntaria ?

R. Neg. quia objectum delectationis est intrinsecus malum, adeoque deliberata delectatio de ea est nala.— *Vol. I. p. 326.*

Is morose delight allowed on a thing prohibited by the law of nature, but here and now having taken place without a formal fault, for instance, delight on nocturnal involuntary pollution?

A. No, because the object of the delight is intrinsically bad, and therefore deliberate delight respecting it is also bad.

Ist moroses Vergnügen an einer Wirkung erlaubt, die durch das Naturrecht verboten ist, aber ohne förmliches Verschulden hin und wieder eintritt, z. B. an unwillkührlicher nächtlicher Pollution?

Antw. Nein; weil der Gegenstand des Vergnügens seinem Wesen nach übel ist, und daher ist vorbedachtes Vergnügen daran böse?

Multi tamen, ut Salmanticenses, Vasquez, Billuart, Antoine, &c., putant quod licet illicitum sit delectari de homicidio, ebrietate, &c., involuntarie commissis, illicitum tamen non sit, ob finem bonum de pollutione mere naturali et involuntaria delectari ; vel affectu simplici et inefficaci eam desideare.

Hujus sententiae etiam est S. Antonius parte 2. tit. 6 cap. 5.

Many, however, as Salman ticenses, Vasquez, Billuart, Antoine &c., think that although it is unlawful to delight on homicide, drunkenness, &c., involuntary committed, it is not unlawful, however, on account of the good end, to delight on merely natural

Viele indessen, wie Salmanticenses, Vasquez, Billuart, Antoine, u. s. w, glauben, daß, obwohl es unerlaubt ist, sich eines Mordes, der Trunkenheit, u. s. w., die unvorsätzlich begangen, zu erfreuen, mit Hinsicht auf den guten Zweck, es doch nicht unerlaubt sei, sich einer

and involuntary pollution or to desire it with a simple and ineffi-cacious affection.

Of this opinion also is Saint Anthony, part 2, tit. 6, chap. 5.

nur natürlichen und unwillkürlichen Pollution zu freuen oder mit un-wirksamer Neigung sie zu wünschen.

Der nämlichen Meinung ist auch St. Antonius, Theil 2. Tit. 6. Kap. 5.

Dicitur "affectu simplici et inefficaci;" quia si desideretur efficaciter, ita ut ex desiderio pollutio causetur, vel media ut eveniat, adhibeantur, certum est juxta omnes quod sit pec-catum mortale. Ratio horum Auctorum est, quod pollutio mere naturalis et involuntaria nullo jure prohibeatur; cum sit effectus mere naturalis, seu mera naturae evacuatio, ut sudor, saliva, &c. ac proinde nequidem materialiter seu ob-jective mala, unde illam ut talem inefficaciter velle non est peccatum.—*Dens, 1. p. 326–7.*

They say "with a simple and inefficacious affection," because if it be desired efficaciously so as that pollution be caused by the desire or means employed that it may happen, it is certain accord-ing to all that it is a mortal sin. The reason of these authors is, that pollution merely natural and involuntary is prohibited by no law; since it is merely a natural effect, or a mere evacuation of nature, like sweat, saliva, &c., and therefore it is by no means materially or objectively bad; whence it is not a sin to wish for it in efficaciously as such.—Dens, v. 1 pp. 326–7.

„Mit einer einfachen und unwirk-samen Neigung" heißt es, weil, wenn wirksam begehrt wird, so, daß durch das Begehren Pollution ver-ursacht wird, oder Mittel angewen-det werden, dieselbe vorzubringen, gewiß ist, daß es eine Todsünde sei. Der Grund dieser Schriftsteller ist, weil die blos natürliche und unwill-kührliche Pollution durch kein Gesetz verboten ist, da sie blos eine natür-liche Wirkung sei, oder eine bloße Entleerung der Natur, wie der Schweiß, Speichel, u. s. w., und daher ist sie weder materiell noch objectiv übel, weßhalb sie als eine solche unwirksam zu wollen, keine Sünde ist.-Dens, Bd. 1. S. 326–7.

Quid est morosa delectatio ?

R. Est voluntaria complacentia circa objectum illicitum absque voluntate implendi seu exequendi opus. — *Vol. I. p. 318–19.*

What is " morose delight ?"
A. It is a voluntary compla-
cence about an illicit object without a wish of performing or exe-
cuting the work.

Was ist das morose Vergnügen?
Es ist ein freiwilliges Wohlge=
fallen an einer unerlaubten Sache,
ohne den Willen des Zustandebrin=
gens oder der Ausführung des
Werks.

Vocatur "morosa" non a mora temporis, quo durat ; nam
unico instanti perfici potest ; sed a mora rationis, quae delectationem hanc, postquam eam advertit, repellere negligit ;
et sic ratio est in mora fungendi suo officio. Potest etiam
dici morosa quia ratio ei immoratur ab que voluntate proce-
dendi ad ipsum opus.—I., 318–19.

It is called " morose," not from
the delay (mora) of time during
which it lasts, for it may be complete in an instant, but from the
delay of reason, which neglects to
repel this delight after it has per-
ceived it ; and thus reason delays
in discharging its own office. It
can also be called "morose," because reason dwells on it without
a wish of proceeding to the work
itself.

Man heißt es moros, was nicht
von einer Verzögerung der Zeit, die
es währ herkommt, denn es kann in
einem Augenblick vollendet werden,
sondern von 'der Zögerung der Ver=
nunft, die dieses Vergnügen, nach=
dem sie dasselbe wahrgenommen hat,
zu unterdrücken versäumt, und so
ist die Vernunft bei der Ausübung
ihrer Pflicht im Verzug. Es kann
auch moros genannt werden, weil
die Vernunft dabei verweilt, ohne
den Willen, zu dem Werk selbst zu
schreiten.

In qua materia haec delectatio locum habet?
R. Quamvis delectatio morosa frequentius contingat circa
venerea, locum tamen habere potest in quacumque materia,
ut circa furtum, pugnam, vindictam, &c.—Dens, T. I. p. 319.

In what matter does this delight
take place ?
A. Although morose delight
more frequently happens about

Bei welcher Materie findet dieses
Vergnügen statt?
Antw. Obwohl das morose Ver=
gnügen sich häufiger bei Sachen,

venereous matters, nowever it can take place in any matter whatsoever, as about theft, about fighting, about revenge, &c.—Dens, vol. 1. p. 319.

bie zur Fleischeslust gehören, zuträgt, so kann es dennoch statthaben auch bei andern Dingen, als: an Stehlen, Raufereien, an der Rache u. s. w.—Dens, Bd. 1. S. 319.

An persona conjugata peccat delectando veneree de copula vel tactibus cum comparte habitis aut habendis, si compars sit absens tempore delectationis infirma, &c., adeo ut copula hic et nunc sit impossibilis?

R. Si delectando se exponat periculo pollutionis, certo pecat mortaliter, contra castitatem, et etiam contra justitiam. Si vero absit periculum pollutionis, Sanchez Sylvius, Steyært, et Daelman eam a mortali liberant, quia honestas status matrimonalis videtur talem delectationem a mortali excusare. Alii tamen probabilius similem delectationem consent mortalem ut Navarrus, Billuart, Collet, Antoine &c.—*Dens, tom. 1. p. 331.*

Does a married person sin in delighting venereously on copulation or on touches, which she has had or is to have, if at the time of the delight her partner be absent or infirm, &c., so as that copulation be here and now impossible?

A. If in delighting she expose herself to the danger of pollution, she certainly sins mortally against chastity, and also against justice. But if there be no danger of pollution, Sanchez, Sylvius, Steyart, and Daelman free her from mortal sin, because the honesty of the matrimonial state seems to excuse such delight from mortal sin. Others, however, as Navarrus, Billuart, Collet, and Antoine &c.

Sündigt eine verheirathete Person durch fleischliches Wohlgefallen an der Paarung oder Berührungen, die sie mit dem Ehegenoß gehabt hat, oder haben wird, wenn derselbe zur Zeit des Wohlgefallens abwesend oder unfähig ist, u. s. w., so daß das Paaren, hier und nun, unmöglich ist?

Wenn sie durch das Vergnügen der Gefahr der Pollution ausgesetzt, so sündigt sie sicherlich gegen die Keuschheit und ebenso gegen das Gesetz. Wenn aber keine Gefahr der Pollution vorhanden ist, so sprechen Sanchez, Sylvius, Steyart und Dälmen sie von der Todsünde frei, weil die Ehrbarkeit des Ehestandes die Schuld der Tod-

think with more probability, that such delight is a mortal sin.— Dens, v. 1. p. 331.

sünde von solchen Vergnügen zu entledigen scheint. Andere glauben mit größerer Wahrscheinlichkeit jedoch, daß ein solches Vergnügen Todsünde sei, wie Navarrus, Viluart, Collet, Antoine, u. s. w.— Dens, Bd. 1. S. 331.

An quispiam voto castitatis obstrictus facit contra suum votum, si aliis personis liberis sit causa libidinis, v. g. si consulat ut illi inter se fornicentur?

R. Peccat peccato scandali, et fit reus fornicationis, aliorum; verumtamen non videtur violare votum proprium mere ob fornicationem aliorum, si absit complacentia propria, quia non vovit servare castitatem alienam, sed propriam, sicuti conjugatus id consulens non peccat contra fidem matrimonii sui.—*Vol. IV. p. 360.*

Does any one bound by a vow of chastity act against his vow if he be the cause of lechery to others, who are free from such vow: for instance, if he advise others to commit fornication with one another?

A. He is guilty of the sin of scandal, and stands arraigned of their fornication; however, he does not seem to violate his own vow merely on account of the fornication of others, if he feel no complacency himself; because he has made no vow to preserve the chastity of others, but his own, just as a married man advising it does not sin against the faith of his matrimony.—Vol. 4. p. 360.

Handelt derjenige, welcher durch das Gelübde der Keuschheit gebunden ist, gegen sein Gelübde, wenn er andern Personen, die von diesem Gelübde frei sind, Veranlassung zur Ausschweifung gibt, z. B., er räth ihnen, daß sie unter sich huren?

Antw. Er sündigt durch die Sünde des Aergernisses und ist ihrer Hurerei schuldig; aber dennoch scheint es, daß er bei der Hurerei Anderer sein Gelübde nicht breche, wenn er nicht selbst Wohlgefallen daran hat, weil er die Keuschheit Anderer zu bewahren nicht gelobt hat, sondern die eigene, gerade wie ein Ehemann, der einen solchen Rath gibt, nicht gegen die eheliche Treue sündigt.— Band 4. S. 360.

Obj. Vovens castitatem vovet non co-operari aut consentire illi peccato contra castitatem.

.R. Id negatur.—*Dens, tom. 4. p. 360.*

Obj. He that makes a vow of chastity, vows not to co-operate with, or consent to, any sin against chastity.

A. That is denied.—Dens, v. 4. p. 360.

Einwendung : Wer Keuschheit gelobt, der gelobt, nicht mitzuwirken oder beizustimmen zu irgend einer Sünde gegen die Keuschheit.

Antw. Das wird geleugnet.— Dens, Bd. 4. S. 360.

Quantum est peccatum exercere actum conjugalem ob solam voluptatem ?

- R. Cum S. Aug. et S. Thom. Supp. p. 49. a. 6. in corp. esse solummodo ex natura sua veniale ; quia haeretur, ut supponitur, in tra limites *legitimi* matrimonii ; potest tamen esse mortale ratione finis, vel aliarum circumstantiarum : puta si v. g. vir itä voluptate captus sit, ut accedens ad uxorum, paratus sit ad eam accedere, licet, uxor non foret, vel si tempore actus conjugalis affectum et delectationem habeat erga aliam, cujus etiam qualitates tunc erunt in confessione exprimenda, puta quod sit conjugata, consanguinea, &c., idque praecipue est cavendum in bigamis, ne dum copulatur conjugi secundae, affectum ponat in priori.—*Vol. VII. p. 182.*

' How great is the sin to exercise the conjugal act solely for pleasure ?

I answer with St. Augustine and St. Thomas (Supp. 40, &c.) that it is only venial in its own nature, because it is fixed as is supposed, within the limits of legitimate matrimony, however it may be a mortal sin by reason of the end, or other circumstances ; suppose, for instance, if the man

Wie groß ist die Sünde, wenn man die eheliche Pflicht blos wegen der Wollust ausübt?

Antw. Nach St. Augustin und St. Thomas, Supp. 49, a. 6. in corp., ist das allein seiner Natur nach erlaubt, weil es, wie angenommen wird innerhalb der Grenzen des rechtmäßigen Ehestandes haftet; es kann zwar eine Todsünde sein, wegen des Endzwecks oder anderer Umstände, als, wenn z. B.

were so seized with pleasure, that going to his wife, he were ready to go to her, though she were not his wife, or if, at the time of the conjugal act, he have his affection and delight towards another, whose qualities also (i. e. as well as the foregoing circumstances) shall then (in that case) be expressed in confession, suppose that she is married, that she is his blood relation, &c., and this is particularly to be guarded against in those who are married a second time, lest, while he is copulating with his second wife, he may fix his affection on the first.—Vol. 7. p. 132.

der Mann so von Wollust ergriffen wäre, daß, indem er zur Frau geht, er bereit wäre, zu ihr zu gehen, wenn sie auch nicht die Ehefrau wäre, oder wenn er zur Zeit der Ausführung der ehelichen Pflicht leidenschaftliche Neigung und Wohlgefallen für eine Andere hätte, deren Eigenschaften alsdann ebenfalls in der Beichte anzuführen sind, z. B. ob sie verheirathet ist, oder mit ihm blutsverwandt u. s. w., und darüber ist besonders zu wachen bei denen, die in zweiter Ehe leben, damit er, indem er seine zweite Frau erkennt, seine leidenschaftliche Zuneigung nicht in die frühere setze. —Band 7. S. 182.

An licet actum conjugalem exercere partim ob debitum finem puta generationem prolis et partim ob delectationem?

R. Negative: quia tunc finis equidem partialiter est inordinatus, cum ex parte obediatur libidini, sicque partialiter invertitur ordo a Deo et natura constitutus.—*Dens, t. 7. p. 182.*

Is it lawful to exercise the conjugal act partly for the due end, namely, the generation of offspring, and partly for delight?

A. No; because then indeed the end is partially inordinate, since in part obedience is given to lust, and thus the order appointed by God and by nature is partially inverted.—Dens, v. 7. p. 182.

Ist es erlaubt, die eheliche Pflicht theilweise des schuldigen Endzwecks wegen, nämlich Erzeugung der Nachkommenschaft, und theilweise des Vergnügens halber auszuüben?

Antw. Nein; weil das Ende davon wenigstens theilweise unordnungsmäßig ist, da zum Theil der Lust gefröhnt, und so die von Gott und der Natur festgestellte Ordnung umgekehrt wird.—Dens, Bd. 7. S. 182.

An licitum est petere debitum conjugale ex solo fine vitandi propriam incontinentiam, non concurrente fine generationis prolis, vel redditionis debiti?

R. Pontius cum multis alliis affirmat, sed melius cum SS Augustino et Thoma videtur negatum.— *Vol. VII. p. 183.*

Is it lawful to ask conjugal duty solely with the end or view of avoiding incontinence in one's self, and without the concurring end of generating offspring or of rendering duty?
A. Pontius and many others say Yes, but it seems better to say No, with St. Augustine and St. Thomas.—Vol. VII. p. 183.

Ob es erlaubt ist, die ehrliche Pflicht zu verlangen blos in der Absicht, der eigenen Unenthaltsamkeit auszuweichen, nicht im Hinblick auf die Beförderung der Nachkommenschaft, oder die Erfüllung einer Pflicht?
Antw. Pontius mit vielen Andern sagt ja, aber nach St. Antonius und St. Thomas scheint es besser zu sein, Nein zu sagen.— Dens, Bd. 7. S. 183.

Conjugatis proponi potest: an pacifice vivant? An honesto modo utantur matrimonia? An periculo pollutionis sese exposerint? An proles Christiane educent?

To the married it can be proposed: whether they live peaceably? Whether they enjoy matrimony in an honest way? Whether they have exposed themselves to the danger of pollution? Whether they bring up their children like Christians?

Eheleuten kann die Frage vorgelegt werden, ob sie im Frieden leben? Ob sie den Ehestand in ehrbarer Weise führen? Ob sie sich der Gefahr der Pollution ausgesetzt haben? Ob sie ihre Nachkommenschaft christlich erziehen?

Circa quae specialiter examinari possunt adolecentes aetatis circiter viginti annorum, sati vegeti et mundani, vel potui dediti?

R. Circa peccata luxuriae primo per generales interrogationes et a longinquo: v. g. an poenitens frequentet personas alterius sexus? Si concedat; an sint dicta quaedam verba inhonesta? Quid secutum? etc. Si negat, potest inquiri : an aliquando vexetur inhonestis cogitationibus vel somniis? Si affirmet, ad interrogationes ulterioris progredi oportet.—*Vol. VI. p. 134.*

About what can young men be specially examined at the age of about twenty years, sufficiently vigorous and like many men of the world, or given to drink ?

A. About the sins of luxury, first by general questions and from afar; for example, whether the penitent frequents persons of the other sex? If he allow that he does; whether any improper words were said? What followed? etc. If he answer in the negative, it can be asked, whether he is at any time tormented with improper thoughts or dreams? If he says Yes, it is fit to proceed to other questions.

Worüber können junge Männer insbesondere gefragt werden, bei einem Alter von etwa zwanzig Jahren, die sehr munterer Natur und weltlich sind, oder dem Trunk ergeben?

Antw. Ueber die Sünde der Ueppigkeit; zuerst durch Fragen im Allgemeinen und von Weitem her, z. B. ob der Beichtende Personen des andern Geschlechts besuche? Wenn er das zugibt, ob manchmal unehrbare Reden geführt werden? Was darauf gefolgt u. s. w. Wenn er verneint, so kann er gefragt werden, ob er mit unehrbaren Gedanken oder Träumen zuweilen belästigt werde? Wenn er das bejaht, so ist nothwendig zu weiteren Fragen zu schreiten.

Eadem prudentiæ forma observabitur circa adolescentulam vel mulierem comptam.—*Dens, t. 6. p. 134.*

The same form of prudence shall be observed about a *young girl* or a *woman* vainly decked.—Dens, v. 6. p. 131.

Die nämliche Art von Vorsicht ist anzuwenden bei dem jungen Mädchen oder der eiteln putzsüchtigen Frau.—Dens, Bd. 6. D. 131.

De Peccatis Carnalibus Conjugum inter se.

Certum est, conjuges inter se peccari posse, etiam graviter contra virtutem castitatis, sive continentiæ, ratione quarundam circumstantiarum; in particulari autem definire, quæ sint mortales, quæ solum veniales, per obscurum est, nec eadem omnium sententia; ut vel ideo sollicite persuadendum sit conjugatis, ut recordentur se esse filios Sanctorum, quos decet in sanctitate conjugali filios procreare. Quidam Auc tores circumstantias circa actum conjugalem præcipue obser-vandas, exprimunt his versibus : *Vo. VII. p. 186.*

<table>
<tr><td>

On the Carnal sins which Man and Wife commit with one another.

It is certain that man and wife can sin grievously against the virtue of chastity or continence, with regard to certain circumstances relating to the use of their bodies ; but to define particularly what are mortal; what only venial, is a matter of very great difficulty, nor are all writers of one opinion on the subject ; so that, even on that account, the married ought to be anxiously advised to recollect that they are the children of the saints, and should therefore beget children in conjugal sanctity. The circumstances which are chiefly to be observed in the performance of the conjugal act, some authors express in the following verses : Vol. VII. p. 186.

</td><td>

Über die Fleischessünde, welche Eheleute unter sich begehen.

Es ist kein Zweifel, daß Eheleute unter sich sündigen können, und sogar schwer, gegen die Tugend der Keuschheit oder Enthaltsamkeit, unter gewissen Umständen; nun aber insbesondere auseinanderzusetzen, was Todsünden und was erläßliche sind, ist sehr schwierig, auch sind die Schriftsteller nicht alle gleicher Meinung hierüber, so, daß deßwegen gerade die Eheleute sorgfältig zu vermahnen sind, zu bedenken, daß sie Kinder der Heiligen seien, denen es gezieme, in Heiligkeit Kinder zu zeugen. Die Umstände, welche vorzugsweise zu beachten sind bei erfüllung der ehlichen Pflicht, drucken einige Schriftsteller in folgenden Sätzen aus:

</td></tr>
</table>

"Sit modus, et finis, sine damno solve, cohære. Sit locus et tempus, tactus, nec spernito votum."

<table>
<tr><td>

[These lines are so extremely obscene that we think it best not to give them in English.]

</td><td>

(Diese zwei Zeilen sind so äusserst schmutzig, daß wir fürs beste halten, dieselben nicht zu übersetzen.)

</td></tr>
</table>

Ergo debet servari modus, sive situs, quia dupliciter invertitur, 1o. si non servetur debitum vas, sed copula, habeatur in vase, sed copula, habeatur in vase præpostero, vel quocumque ali non naturali; quod semper mortale est spectans a l sodomiam minorem, seu imperfectam, idque tenendum contra, quosdam laxistas, sive copula ibi consummetur sive tantum inchoetur consummanda in vase naturali.—Vol. VII. p. 186.

Therefore method or posture ought to be observed, which is inverted in a two fold way: 1st, when the proper passage or vessel is not kept, but the connection takes place in the hinder passage or vessel, or in any other not ordained by nature for that purpose, which is always a mortal sin, tending to that which is called minor* or imperfect sodomy, and

Daher follte die Art und Weife und die Lage beobachtet werden, weil es auf zweierlei Weife verkehrt wird: 1. Wenn daß gebührende Gefäß nicht eingehalten wurde, fondern die Verbindung in dem hintern Gefäße stattfände, oder in irgend einem andern, welches nicht das naturliche, was töbliche Sünde ist und auf die geringe, oder unvollkommene Sodomie*) abzieht,

Quid est sodomia perfecta?

R. Est congressus carnalis inter personas ejusdem sexus, nimirum masculi cum masculo, feminæ cum femina, in quocunque vase congressus fiat.

Sodomia imperfecta sive sodomia minor est congressus carnalis maris cum femina, sed extra vas femineum naturale, v. g. si vir offundat semen suum retro per anum in intestinum stercoreum feminæ. Dens, tom. 4. p. 362.

*MINOR SODOMY.—In the fourth volume he divided sodomy into two species, perfect or imperfect, or minor.

What is perfect sodomy?

ANSWER.—It is carnal congress between persons of the same sex, namely, of a male with a male, of a female with a female, in whatever vessel the congress may take place.

Imperfect or minor sodomy is the carnal congress of a male with a female, but without the natural vessel of the female, for instance, if a man discharge his semen behind through the anus into the stercoreous intestines of the woman. —Dens, v. 4, p. 362.

*) Geringere Sodomie.— Im vierten Bande theilte er die Sodomie in zwei Gattungen ein, in vollkommene und in unvollkommene oder geringere Sodomie.

Was ist die vollkommene Sodomie?

Antw. Es ist ein fleischliches Zusammenkommen von Perfonen des gleichen Geschlechts, nämlich männlicher mit männlichen und weiblicher mit weiblichen, in was immer für einem Gefäß das Zusammenkommen geschehe.

Unvollkommene oder geringere Sodomie ist das fleischliche Zusammenkommen des Ehemannes mit der Frau außerhalb des natürlichen weiblichen Gefäßes, wenn z. B. der Mann feinen Samen hinten durch den After in den Kothdarm der Frau ausgießt.—Den, Bd. 4. S. 362.

this must be held against certain Divines of loose opinions, whether the connection be consummated in the natural passage.—Vol. 7. p. 186.

und das muß gewissen schlaffen Theologen entgegengehalten wer= den, ob die Verbindung dort voll= endet, oder begonnen, um im natür= lichen Gefäß vollendet zu werden.

Modus sive situs invertitur ut servetur debitum vas ad copulam a natura ordinatum, v. g. si fiat accedendo præpostero, a latere, stando, vel si vir sit succumbus. Modus is mortalis est si inde suboriatur periculum pollutionis respectu alterutrius quando periculum est, ne semen perdatur, prout sæpe accidit, dum actus exercetur stando, sedendo, aut viro succumbente : Si absit et sufficienter præcaveatur istud periculum, ex communi sententia id non est mortale : est autem veniale ex gravioribus, cum sit inversio ordinis naturæ; est que generatim modus ille sine causa taliter coeundi graviter a Confessariis reprehendendus : si tamen ob justam rationem situm naturalem conjuges immutent, secludaturque dictum periculum nullum est peccatum, ut dictum est in numero 48. Vol. VII. p. 186.

Method of posture is inverted, though the connection take place in the passage or vessel appointed by nature for that purpose, for instance, if it be done by an attack from behind, or when the parties are on their sides, or standing or sitting, or when the husband lies underneath his wife. This method of doing it is a *mortal* sin, if there should therefrom arise to either party a danger of pollution, or of losing the seed, a thing which *often happens* when the act is per-

Die Art und Weise oder die Lage wird verkehrt, im Falle das gehö= rige, von der natur angeordnete Ge= fäß auch eingehalten wurde, wenn es z. B. durch das Hinzutreten von hinten geschieht, oder von der Seite, im Stehen, Sitzen, oder wenn der Mann unten liegt. Diese Art und Weise ist Todsünde, wenn davon in Beziehung auf eines der Theilneh= mer die Gefahr der Pollution ent= steht, oder wenn Gefahr ist, daß Same verloren gehe, wie es sich oft ereignet, wenn der Act im Stehen,

formed standing, or sitting or the husband lying underneath ; but if that danger be sufficiently guarded against, it is not, in the common opinion of Divines, a mortal sin: yet it is one of the weighter sort of venial sins, since it is an inversion of the order of nature; and in general, that method of thus coming to coition must when without sufficient cause be severely censured by the Confessors: if, however, man and wife, for some just reason, change the natural posture, and if the aforesaid danger (of losing the seed) be secluded, there will be no sin, as has been said in number 48.—Vol. VII. p. 186.

Sitzen, ober der Mann unten liegend vollzogen wird; wenn aber diese Gefahr nicht vorhanden wäre, oder derselben genugend vorgebeugt würde, so ist es nach der allgemeinen theologischen Meinung keine Todsünde; es ist jedoch eine der schwereren erläßlichen Sünden, da es ein Verkehren der Ordnung der Natur ist, und im Allgemeinen ist jene Art und Weise des Zusammengehens, ohne Ursache, von den Beichtvätern streng zu tadeln; wenn indessen aus gerechtem Grund Eheleute die natürliche Lage ändern, und besagte Gefahr vermieden wird, so ist es keine Sünde, wie No. 48 gesagt worden ist. Bd. 7. S. 186.

An uxor posset se tactibus exitare ad seminationem, si a copula conjugali se retraxerit, maritus, postquam ipse seminavit,   sed antequam seminaverit uxor.

R. Plurimi negant ; eo quod, cum vir se retraxerit, actus sit completus, adeoque illa seminatio mulieris foret peccatum pollutionis: alii vero affirmant : quia ista excitatio spectat ad actus conjugalis complementum et perfectionem ; excipeunt tamen casum, ubi periculum est ne semen ad extra profundatur.—Vol. VII. 188.

Can a wife by touches excite herself to spend, if the husband has withdrawn himself from conjugal copulation, after he has spent himself, but before the wife has spent.

A. Very many say no ; because

Ob sich die Frau durch Betasten zum Samenlassen aufreizen könne, wenn sich der Mann von der ehelichen Paarung zurückgezogen, nachdem er selbst Samen gelassen hat, aber vorher ehe die Frau den Samen ließ?

when the husband has withdrawn himself, the act is complete, and therefore that spending of the woman would be a sin of pollution; but others say yes; because that artificial mode of excitement tends to the completion and perfection of the conjugal act; they, however, except the case where there is canger lest the seed may be poured forth from the outside. V. VII. p. 188.

Antw. Die meisten verneinen es; weil, wenn der Mann sich zurückgezogen hat, der Akt vollzogen zei, und daher alles Samenlassen der Frau die Sünde der Pollution wäre; andere aber bejahen es, weil diese Aufreizung auf die Vervollständigung und Vollendung des ehelichen Akts abzielt; sie nehmen jedoch den Fall aus, wo Gefahr ist, daß der Same nach aussen ausgeschüttet werde. Bd. 7. S. 188.

Hanc posteriorem sententiam ad exorbitantes opiniones laxiorum refert Henricus a S. Ignatio.—*Tom VII. p. 188.*

Henricus, from St. Ignatius, refers this last opinion to the exhorbitant opinions of the more lax Divines. Vol. VII. p. 188.

Henricus verweist diesen letzteren gelehrten Ausspruch von St. Ignatius unter die ausschweifenden Ansichten der schlafferen Theologen. Bd. 7. S. 188.

EXTRACTS

FROM BISHOP KENRICK'S THEOLOGY.

Auszüge aus den Theologie des Bischof Kenrick.

152. Fellatores vocat Martialis "lingua maritos et ore mœchos." (L. xi. epigr. 61.) Pessimum hoc libidinis genus mortale esse et naturæ repugnare liquet. Qui linguam mulieris os immittunt, in proximo pollutionis discrimine versantur, et contra naturam voluptatem quærere convincuntur: quapropter nequeunt a lethali eximi culpa, nisi obiter fiat, absque venerea delectatione. —T. I. p. 130.

152. Martialis defines the suckers as "adulterers with the tongue, and adulteresses with the mouth." That this vile description of lust involves mortal sin and is repugnant to nature, is manifest. They who thrust the tongue into the mouth of a woman are in extreme danger of pollution, and are convicted of seeking pleasure in an unnatural manner; and therefore they cannot be exempt from deadly sin, unless it be done without design and without sensual gratification.

152. Martialis heißt die Sauger "Ehmänner mit der Zunge und Ehebrecher mit dem Munde." (B. 11. Epigr. 61.) Daß diese ärgste Art von Ausschwefung Todsünde und ganz naturwidrig sei, ist klar. Diejenigen, welche ihre Zunge in den Mund von Weibspersonen stecken, sind in der nächsten Gefahr, der Pollution und des Verbrechens schuldig, gegen die Naturgesetze ihre Wollust zu befriedigen gesucht zu haben; daher auch solche von der Todsünde nicht freigesprochen werden können, außer wenn es ohne die Absicht des wollüstigen Genusses geschehen wäre.

VOLUME III. PAGE 308

§ *II. De usu conjugii.*

67. Conjugii usus, modo rationi convenienti, licitus est, nam ex ipso Conditoris instituto fit ut maris et feminæ conjunctione genus propagetur humanum. "Situs naturalis est, ut mulier sit succuba, et vir incubus; hic enim modus aptior est effusioni seminis virilis, et receptioni in vas femineum ad prolem procreandam. Situs autem innaturalis est si coitus aliter fiat, nempe sedendo, stando, de latere, vel præpostere more pecudum, vel si vir sit succubus, et mulier, incuba."—*L. VI. n. 917.*

Of the use of Marriage.

67. The use of marriage, in a manner agreeably to reason, is lawful, for from the institution of the Creator it is appointed that the human species shall be propagated by the union of the male and the female. "The natural position is that the woman should be under and the man on top, for this position is better adapted for the effusion of the seed of the male and for its reception into the female vessel for the propagation of offspring. But an unnatural position is, if an union be effected in any other way—as sitting, standing, or on the side, or behind after the manner of beasts, or if the man shall be under and the woman on top."

§ II. Über den Gebrauch des Ehestandes.

67. Der Gebrauch des Ehstands in einer vernünftigen Weise ist erlaubt, denn nach der Anordnung des Schöpfers selbst soll durch die Verbindung von Mann und Frau das Menschengeschlecht fortgepflanzt werden. "Die natürliche Lage ist, daß der Mann oben und der Frau unten liege; diese Art ist nämlich für die Ausgießung des männlichen Samens und die Empfängniß desselben im weiblichen Gefäß die zur Kindererzeugung geeignetere. Eine unnatürliche Lage aber ist es, wenn die Begattung in andere Weise vor sich geht, als sitzend, stehend, von der Seite oder von hinten nach Art des Viehs, oder wenn der Mann unten liegt und die Frau oben."(B. 6. N. 917.)

68. Si conjuges incœpta copula, ex mutuo consensu cohibeant seminationem absque effusionis periculo, per se non est peccatum mortale. * * * *

68. If married persons, in the act of copulation, restrain by mutual consent the emission of seed without the danger of spilling it, it is not in itself a mortal sin. *
* * * *

68. Wenn verheirathete Personen mit gegenseitiger Einwilligung die Besamung hindern, ohne die Gefahr des Verschüttens, so ist das keine Todsünde an und für sich. *
* * * *

69. "Si vero fœmina jam seminaverit, vel sit in probabili periculo seminandi, non potest quidem vir data opera a seminatione se retrahere, sine gravi culpa, quia tunc ipse est cau sa, ut semen uxoris prodigatur." (L. vi. n. 918.)

69. But if the woman has now spent her seed, or is in probable danger of spending, the man cannot draw back from spending his seed, having begun the work, without a grievous fault, because he is then the cause that the seed of the woman is thrown away.

69. Wenn aber die Frau ihren Samen schon gelassen hat, oder die Gefahr, daß sie denselben lassen werde wahrscheinlich ist, so kann sich der Mann, da er hierauf hingewirkt hat, von der Besamung nicht zurückziehen, ohne schwere Verschuldung; indem er alsdann Veranlassung gegeben hat, daß der Same der Frau verloren gegangen. (B. 6. N. 918.)

70. Si vir jam seminaverit, femina retrahendo se a seminando plerisque videtur peccare lethaliter, quia juxta plures utrumque semen ad generationem requiritur.

70. If the man have now spent his seed, the woman by withdrawing herself from spending her seed for many reasons appears to commit a deadly sin, because according to many the seed of both is required for generation.

70. Hat der Mann bereits Samen gelassen, so sündigt, nach der Meinung Vieler, die Frau töblich, wenn sie sich von der Besamung zurückzieht, denn Viele sind der Ansicht, daß der Same von beiden zur Zeugung erforderlich sei.

73. Peccat mortaliter vir copulam inchoando in vase præpostero, ut postea in vase debito eam consummet. Ita com-
munius et verius sentiunt theologi. "Ratio quia ipse hujusmodi coitus (etsi absque seminatione) est vera sodomia, quamvis non consummata, sicut ipsa copula in vase naturali mulieris alienæ est vera fornicatio licet non adsit seminatio." Vi-
rilia perfricare circa vas præposterum uxoris est etiam mortale; "ratio est quia saltem talis tactus non potest moraliter
fieri sine affectu sodomitico."—L. vi. n. 916.)

' 73. A man commits a deadly sin who begins copulation in the posterior vessel (fundament) and afterwards finishes it in the proper vessel. Theologians agree generally in this. "The reason is that a connection of this kind (although without the emission of seed) is real sodomy, although not consummated, as copulation itself in the natural vessel of another woman is true fornication, though no seed was spent." For a man to rub his penis all around the fundament of his wife is a mortal sin; the reason is because such touching at least cannot be done, morally speaking, without a sodomitical effect.

73. Ein Mann sündigt tödlich, der die Verpaarung im hintern Ge= fäß anfängt, um dernach dieselbe in dem gehörigen Gefäß zu beendigen. Darin stimmen im Allgemeinen die wahren Theologen überein. "Der Grund ist der, weil eine solche fleisch= liche Vermischung (wenn auch ohne Besamung) wahre Sodomie ist, wenn auch nicht vollendete, sowie auch das Verpaarung im natürliches Gefäß mit einer andern Weibsper= son wahre Hurerei ist, wenn auch keine Besamung stattfindet." Die männlichen Geschlechtstheile um das hintere Gefäß der Frau ist auch Todsünde, aus dem Grunde, weil solches Tasten nicht moralisch ge= schehen kann ohne Sodomitischen Affect. (Bd. 6. N. 916.)

79. In loco sacro copula habenda non est, extra necessi-
tatem, quæ contingit exercitu in ecclesia diversante.

79. Copulation is not to be performed in a sacred place, ex-cept through necessity, which may

79. An einem heiligen Orte soll die Begattung nicht statthaben ohne Noth, was der Fall sein kann, wenn

happen when an army is lodging in the church.   eine Militärbesatzung in einer Kirche kampirt.

81. Coire tamen cum prægnante S. Alphonso videtur culpa venialis, "nisi adsit periculum incontinentiæ, vel alia honesta casa."—(S. Alph. 1. vi. n. 924.)

81. To have connection with a pregnant woman, to S. Alphonso it appears a venial sin, unless there is danger of incontinency, or some other proper cause.

81. Mit einer schwangern Frau sich fleischlich vermischen, scheint dem S. Alphonso erläßliche Sünde zu sein, "außer, wenn die Gefahr der Unenthaltsamkeit, oder eine andere ehrbare Ursache vorhanden ist."
(S. Alph. 1. vi. N. 924.)

ᵠ 92. Non debet vir jejuniis nimiis se reddere impotentem, nec mulier jejunando fieri nimis deformis, adeo ut eam vir aversetur.

92. A man should not render himself impotent by too much fasting, nor should a woman by fasting become so deformed that a man would turn away from her.

92. Der Mann soll sich nicht durch allzuvieles Fasten unfähig machen, ebenso sollte die Frau sich nicht durch übermäßiges Fasten so verunstalten, daß dem Manne vor ihr eckelt.

95. Si actus sit venialiter malus, S. Alphonsus sic distinguit : "actus est illicitus ex parte petentis, puta si petat ob voluptatem, vel alium finem leviter malum, vel die quo vult Eucharistiam accipere, tunc tenetur reddere ; quia, cum actus sit per se honestus, tenetur ex justitia ad reddendum, etiamsi exigens peccet graviter in petendo, ut diximus n. 944. Dub. 1. Si vero actus est venialiter illicitus ex parte ipsius actus, seu copulæ, ut si petatur situ innaturali, vel tempore menstrui, aut puerperii, tunc quando adest justacausa, potest quidem reddere, cum quælibet justa causa excuset a veniali. Justa autem causa erit, v. g. ne incurrat in-

dignationem alterius, sive rancorem illius quodammodo
notabilem, et non possit cum commode avertere. . . .
Dixi, *potest reddere*, sed non tenetur, quia licet vinculum
justitiæ fortius sit vinculo charitatis, attamen cum actus, sit
tali modo per se illicitus, alter non habet jus ad illum." (L.
vi. n. 946.)

95. If an act is venially bad, S. Alphonsus makes this distinction: "The act is unlawful on the part of him who seeks it, that is if he seek it on account of carnal pleasure, or for any other purpose, slightly wrong; or on the day in which he wishes to receive the Eucharist, *then he is bound to render* (the duty); because when the act is *proper † in itself*, he is bound by justice to render (to pay), although exacting it he may sin grievously in asking it, as we have said N. 944. Dub. 1. But if the act be venially unlawful (illicit) on the part of the act itself, or of copulation, as if it may be sought in an unnatural posture, or in the time of menstruation, or of parturition, then when a just cause is present, he can render (the duty); because any just cause will excuse from venial sin. It will be just cause, v. g. lest he should incur the indignation of another, or the malice of one in any way notable, and can-

95. Wann ein Akt erläßlich böse sei, erklärt S. Alphonso also:

"Der Akt ist unerlaubt auf Seite dessen, der ihn begehrt, nämlich wenn er aus Wollust denselben verlangt, oder zu einem andern erläßlich bösen Zweck; oder an dem Tage, an dem er das h. Abendmhal nehmen will, dann ist er zwar verbunden, die eheliche Pflicht zu erfüllen, weil der Akt an und für sich ehrbar ist, und er also mit Recht verbunden ist, die Pflicht zu leisten, wenn er aber den Akt selbst hervorruft, sündigt er schwer durch dieses Begehren, wie wir N. 944 Dub. 1 gesagt haben. Wenn aber der Akt erläßlich unerlaubt ist, des Akts selbst wegen, oder der Begattung, als, wenn derselbe im unnatürlichen Gefäß begehrt wird, oder zur Zeit der Reinigung oder des Wochenbetts, dann wenn eine gerechte Ursache vorhanden ist, so kan er die eheliche Pflicht allerdings leisten, weil irgend eine gerechte Ursache von der erläßlichen Sünde entschuldigt. Gerechte Ursache, z. B., ist es, wenn

---

* Tunc tenetur reddere.
† Honestus per se.

not fitly avert it. I have said *he can render it*, but he is not bound, because although the bond* (obligation) of justice may be stronger than the bond of love, yet when an act may be in such a manner illicit in itself, the other has no right to it...

er sich die Unzufriedenheit des Andern zuziehen wurde, oder dessen gewissenmaßen auffallenden Groll, den er sonst nicht schicklich vermeiden könnte... . Wie ich gesagt habe, er kann die Pflicht leisten, aber er ist nicht dazu verbunden, weil, obgleich die Verbindlichkeit des Rechts stärker ist, als die der Liebe, dennoch, wenn ein derartiger Akt unerlaubt ist, der andere Theil kein Recht darauf hat." (B. vi. N.946.)

96. Si homo extra vas seminaturus noscatur, utrum uxor possit eum excipere inquiritur. Equidem constat eam non posse id consillii, quum detestandum, sit, probare : sed excusant eam plures, eum excipientem, quia copula inchoata per se licet, et quod seminatio extra fiat, culpa aliena contingit. Cæterum quotiescumque possit precibus et monitis eum inducere ut coitum integrum habeat, videter teneri : nec facile excusatur si ipsa absque gravi causa petat debitum, quando novit eum ita rem habiturum, nam ex charitate tenetur impedire peccatum viri : "justam autem causam habet petendi, si ipsa esset in periculo, incontinentiæ, vel si deberet alias privari suo jure petendi plusquam semel, vel bis, cum perpetuo scrupulo an ci sit satis grave incommodum, vel ne, nunc se continere."—L. vi. n. 947.

96. If a man may know that he is about to drop his seed without the female vessel, it is inquired whether the wife can receive him. Indeed it is evident she cannot prove that it is a thing designed,

86. Wenn einer Mann weiß, daß er seinen Samen ausserhalb des Gefäßes abläßt, so fragt es sich ob sie ihn zu sich lassen könne. Zwar ist richtig, sie kann nicht beweisen, daß er es absichtlich thue, da es verab-

* Vin culum.

seeing it is to be detested. But many excuse her for receiving him, for copulation begun is lawful in itself, and because the seed may be dropped without, it may happen from another cause, another fault may happen culpa aliena contingit. But as often as she can by prayers and counsels induce him to have with her a perfect copulation, it appears he should be retained; nor is she easily excused if she, without a weighty reason, seeks the (matrimonial) debt, when she knows he is about to have the matter so, for from charity she is bound to hinder the sin of the man. "But she has a just cause for asking it, if she is in danger of incontinency or if she ought otherwise to be deprived of her right of asking more than once or twice with continual doubt whether it may be a sufficiently great inconvenience to her or not, now to contain herself."

ſchenungswürdig iſt, aber Viehle entſchuldigen ſie, wenn ſie ihn zuläßt, weil die Begattung beim Beginn an und für ſich erlaubt iſt, und ſie an der Urſache, aus welcher der Same verloren geht, keine Schuld trägt. Indeſſen ſo oft ſie durch Bitten und Ermahnen ihn bewegen kann, die Begattung vollſtändig mit ihr zu haben, ſo ſcheint ſie verpflichtet zu ſein, das zu thun; ebenſo kann ſie nicht leicht entſchuldigt werden, wenn ſie ohne wichtige Gründe die eheliche Pflicht verlangt, während ſie weiß, daß er die Sache ſo betreibt, denn ſie muß aus Liebe den Mann vor Sünde zu bewahren ſuchen; "gerechte Urſache aber hat ſie, die Pflicht zu verlangen, wenn ſie ſelbſt der Gefahr der Unenthaltſamkeit ausgeſetzt iſt, da ſie ſonſt ihres Recht beraubt wurde, öfterer wie ein oder zweimal die eheliche Pflicht zu verlangen, ohne beſtändige Zweifel, ob es unter ſolchen Umſtänden ein völlig genügendes Hinderniß gibt, ſich zu enthalten. (B. d. N. 947.)

97. Non tenetur reddere debitum conjugi qui remisit jus suum, v. g. castitatem vovendo ex consensu mutuo. Quod si ita co senserit, ut non cesserit suo juri, tunc instanter petenti videtur reddendum, quum per se debeatur, et alter suo jure non ceciderit bono voluntatis proposito. Amenti reddendum non est debitum, quum dominii usus ratione indigeat. Attamen si non sit omnino mente captus, licet ei petenti ob-

temperare præsertim ne prodigatur semen, quando ex coitu nullum incommodum grave timendum sit. Cum muliere amente non licet coire, nisi sterilis noscatur, proli enim inferretur damnum. Peccaret qui conjuges amentes conjungeret ad copulam, quum proles careret necessaria educatione.

97. The woman is not bound to render the matrimonial duty to the husband who has thrown away his right by vowing chastity with mutual consent. Because if it should be so agreed, that he may not have yielded his right, then instantly it appears that it should be rendered to the one asking when it is due (per se) in itself, and the other may not have fallen from her right with a good purpose of will. The debt is not to be paid to one that is demented, since the use of authority needs reason.—Nevertheless, if one is not altogether lost in mind, it is lawful to comply with the person asking, especially lest the seed should be thrown away when from copulation no great disadvantage is to be dreaded. It is not lawful to copulate with a woman who is a fool, unless it be known that she is barren, for an injury is brought upon the offspring. He sins who shall unite foolish persons together to copulate, seeing their offspring will lack a proper education.

97. Wer, durch gelobte gegenseittge Keuschheit z. B., sein Recht aufgegeben hat, ist nicht verbunden, die eheliche Pflicht zu leisten. Wenn er in der Art zugestimmt hat, daß er sein Recht nicht aufgebe, dann scheint es, daß er dem andern Theil, der die Pflicht verlangt, dieselbe unverzüglich leisten muß, da er dieses selbstverständlich schuldig ist, und der andere Theil sein Recht in keiner guten Willensabsicht aufgegeben hat. Die Pflicht ist keinem zu leisten, der den Verstand verloren hat, denn die Ausübung eines Rechts setzt den Besitz der Vernunft voraus. Wenn indessen einer den Verstand nicht gänzlich verloren hat, so ist es erlaubt, seinem Verlangen zu entsprechen, haubptsächlich deßwegen, damit der Samen nicht verloren gehe, vorausgesetzt, daß kein bedeutender Nachtheil zu befurchten ist. Es ist nicht erlaubt, sich mit einer Frau zu begatten, die den Verstand verloren hat, ausser wenn sie als unfruchtbar bekannt ist, den der Nachkommenschaft wurde daraus Schaden entspringen. Derjenige sündigt, der verstandeslose Eheleute zur Begattung zusammenbringt, da es deren

Kinder an der nöthigen Erziehung fehlen würde.

98. Non tenetur conjux debitum reddere alteri adulterii reo, fides enim semel fracta alterum obligatione solvit, manente tamen conjugii vinculo. Igitur si de delicto constet, vel vehementia sint ejus indicia culpanda non est uxor quæ renuit subesse marito.

98. Nor is one party bound to render the matrimonial debt to another guilty of adultery; for faith once broken frees the other from obligation, though the bond of marriage still remains. If therefore there is evidence of direliction, or if the evidences of it are very strong, the wife is not to be blamed if she refuse to submit to the husband.

98. Kein Ehgatte ist verbunden, dem andern die Eheliche Pflicht zu leisten, der des Ehebruchs schuldig ist, denn wenn die Treue einmal gebrochen wird, so ist der andere Theil seiner Pflicht ledig, auch wenn das Eheband noch nicht aufgelöst ist. Ist daher der Beweis eines solchen Verhens vorhanden, oder starke Anzeichen der Schuld, so ist die Frau nicht zu tadeln, wenn sie es abweist, dem Manne Folge zu leisten.

99. Ebrio non tenetur conjux morem gerere, caret enem usu rationis, qui ad exercendum dominium requiritur. Quod si non adeo ebrius sit ut nequeat rem habere, licet utique obtemperare, quamvis vix teneatur. Ad impediendum dissidia rixas, et blasphemias plerumque oportet petenti acquiescere : quod si contingat effundi extra vas semen, id ebrio imputandum erit.

99. Nor is the spouse held to obey a drunken husband, for he lacks the use of reason, which is required for the exercise of authority. But if he is not so drunk that he can do the thing, she is free then to yield, although she is scarcely bound. For the sake of

99. Ebenso wenig ist die Frau verbunden, einem betrunkenen Ehemanne zu gehorchen, denn er ist nicht im Gebrauch seiner Vernunft, die ihm zur Ausübung seiner ehelichen Rechte erforderlich ist. Wenn er jedoch nicht so sehr betrunken ist, daß er das Ding thun kann, so ist

preventing separations, strifes, blasphemies, most commonly it becomes her to yield to him asking; but if it should happen that the seed is omitted outside of the female vessel, that will be imputed to the drunkard.

L.

ihr erlaubt, ihn zuzulassen, obwohl sie dazu kaum verbunden ist. Um Zwistigkeiten, Zänkereien und Gotteslästerungen zu vermeiden, ist es für sie angemessen, seinem Begehren zu entsprechen; allein wenn sich ergeben sollte, daß der Same ausserhalb des weiblichen Gesäßes verschüttet wird, so liegt die Schuld am Säufer.

100. Qui ob incestum privatus est jure petendi debiti, tenetur nihilominus ad reddendum: nec enim alter ob ejus culpam puniendus est. Qui castitatem vovit, absque conjugis consensu, pariter tenetur reddere, quamvis nequeat petere, nam non potuit conjugis jus afficere suæ voluntatis proposito.

100. Whoever on account of incest is deprived by law of seeking the (matrimonial) debt he is held, nevertheless, to render it; for neither is another person to be punished for his fault. He who vows chastity without the consent of his spouse, is in like manner held to render (the duty), although he cannot seek it, for he cannot effect the right of the spouse (conjugis) by a resolution of his will.

100. Wer wegen Bluthschande des Rechts gesetzlich verlustig geworden ist, die eheliche Pflicht zu verlangen, ist gleichwohl verbunden, dieselbe zu leisten, indem der andere Theil für die Schuld desselben nicht bestraft werden kann. Wer Keuschheit Gelobt, ohne die Zustimmung seines Gatten, ist gleichfalls verbunden, die eheliche Pflicht zu leisten, wenn er dieselbe auch schon nicht verlangen kann, denn er kann das Recht der Frau nach seinem Willen nicht einseitig verkurzen.

101. Conjuges tenentur ad reddendum debitum cum levi suo incommodo et damno, nam conjugio ineundo, se obligarunt ad ea quæ huic insunt. Si contingat alterutrum morbo aliquo laborare, qui contagiosus non sit, non debet alter ejus effugere consortium, nam et leproso debitum reddendum est.

Quod si infectio timenda sit, ex medicorum judicio, vel si conjux sanus vehementer abhorreat ab alterius consortio, excusandus videtur, impossibilium enim nulla est obligatio.

101. Married Persons are bound to render the duty (even if it snould be) at their trifling inconvenience and loss, for marriage being entered into, they obligate themselves to those things which are connected with it. If it should happen that the one or the other labors under any disease, which is not contagious, the other ought not to shun his companion, for the debt is to be rendered to a leper. Whereas, if infection is feared, from the opinion of physicians, or if the partner will vehemently abhor the intercourse of the other, he appears to be excused, for the obligation of impossible things is null, and there is no obligation to do impossible things.

101. Verheirathete Personen sind verbunden, die eheliche Pflicht zu leisten, auch wenn das ihnen leichte Unbequemlichkeiten oder Schaden zufugt, denn damit, daß sie die Ehe eingegangen, haben sie sich zu dem verbindlich gemacht, was die Ehe mit sich bringt. Wenn der eine oder andere Gatte an einer Krankheit leidet, die nicht anstecken ist, so kann sich keiner von ihnen seinem Gemahl entziehen, denn selbst einem Aussätzigen muß die eheliche Pflicht geleistet werden. Wenn aber Ansteckung zu befürchten ist nach dem Ausspruch der Ärzte, oder wenn der gesunde Gatte einen heftigen Abscheu vor dem andern hat, so scheint es, daß er zu entschuldigen ist, denn zu Unmöglichem ist Niemand verbunden.

103. Uxor quæ experta est se non posse parere absque vitæ periculo, non tenetur reddere debitum, nam cum tanto sui detrimento nequit obligari : attamen potest reddere, nam licet illi se objicere periculo quod ex sui conditione oritur, præsertim si id ad vitandam sui, vel conjugis incontinentiam necessarium sit. Si semper pariat filios mortuos, plures dicunt eam posse reddere, quamvis non teneatur, nam præstet infantes esse, etiam cum peccato originis, quam non esse, et per accidens eorum mors contingit, quum conjugii usus per se licitus sit. Ego distinguendum puto. Si fœtus mors in

utero contingat, vel alias, absque actu chirurgi vitam tollentis, uti que videtur licere uti matrimonio, etsi prævideatur eventura : sed si fœtum forcipibus tollendum constet, dubitari posset utrum liceat conjugio uti, cum tanto prolis detrimento.   Equidem optandum ut abstinerent conjuges ; sed quum incontinentiæ sit periculum, excusari forsan poterunt, chirurgorum permittentes arbitrio, quomodo cum uxore parturiente agendum sit.—*T. III. p. 317.*

103. A wife who has experienced that she cannot bear children without danger of her life, is not held to render the duty, for she cannot be obligated under such personal damage ; nevertheless she can render it, for it is lawful for her to subject herself to the danger, which arises from her condition, especially if it is necessary for the avoiding of her own incontinence or her husband's. If she always have brought forth dead children, many say that she can render it, although she is not (bound) held, for it is better that there should be children, even with the sin of the beginning, than that there should be no children and their death happens by an accident, while the use of marriage is lawful in itself. I think we must distinguish. If the death of the child should happen in the womb, or elsewhere, without the act of the surgeon taking away its life, and as it appears lawful to use the marriage right, although

103. Eine Frau, welche die Erfahrung gemacht hat, daß sie nicht ohne Lebensgefahr Kinder gebären könne, ist nicht verbunden, die eheliche Pflicht zu leisten, bei einer solchen persönlichen Gefahr kann sie nicht verbindlich gemacht werden; jedoch ist es ihr erlaubt, der Gefahr sich auszusetzen, die aus ihrer persönlichen Beschaffenheit entsteht, wenn dieses zur Vermeidung ihrer eigenen Unenthaltsamkeit oder der ihres Mannes nöthig ist. Wenn sie immer todte Kinder gebiert, so glauben Viele, daß sie die Pflicht leisten könne, obwohl sie nicht dazu verbunden ist, denn es ist besser, daß Kinder erzeugt werden, selbst mit der Erbsünde, als daß nicht, und ihr Tod ereignet sich zufällig, während der Gebrauch des Ehestandes an und für sich erlaubt ist. Ich glaube man muß einen unterschied machen.   Wenn der Tod des Kindes in Mutterleibe erfolgt, oder sonst wo, ohne daß es durch die Behandlung Geburtshelfers das Leben verliert, und da es als erlaubt er-

the event may be foreseen; but if the child has to be removed by the forceps,.it is doubtful whether it is right to use the marriage right with so much danger of the offspring. Indeed, it is believed that married persons would abstain, but when there is danger of incontinence, perhaps they can be excused, they leaving it to the will of the surgeons how they must act with a woman in labor.

fcheint, fich des ehelichen Rechts zu bedienen, obschon das Ergebniß voraußgefehen ift; wenn dagegen das Kind mit der Zange genommen werden muß, fo ift es zweifelhaft, ob es bei fo großer Gefahr für die Nachkommenfchaft erlaubt fei, das eheliche Recht zu gebrauchen. Es ift in der That wünfchenswerth, daß die Eheleute von der Außübung der Pflicht abstehen, wenn aber die Gefahr der Unenthaltfamkeit vorhanden ift, fo können fie vielleicht entfchuldigt werden, es dem Urtheile der Geburtshelfer überlaffend, wie die gebärende Frau zu behandeln fei. (B. 3. S. 317.)

104. Uxor quæ in usu matrimonii se vertit, ut non recipiat semen, vel statim post illud exceptum surgit, ut expellatur, lethaliter peccat; sed opus non est ut diu resupina jaceat, quum matrix brevi semen attrahat, et mox arctissime claudatur. Puellæ vim patienti licet se vertere, et conari, ut non recipiat semen, quod injuria ei immittitur: sed exceptum non licet expellere, quia jam possessionem pacificam habet, et haud absque injuria naturæ ejiceretur.—*T. III. p. 317.*

104. The wife who turns herself in the act of connection that she may not receive the seed, or rises up immediately after it has been received, that it may be expelled, sins mortally. But there is no need that she should lie a long time on her back, seeing that the womb attracts the seed in a

104. Eine Frau fündigt töblich, wenn fie fich beim Begatten wendet, fo daß fie den Samen nicht empfangen möge, oder wenn fie, nachdem fie den Samen empfangen hat, fogleich auffteht, um denfelben außzufchütten. Indeffen ift es nicht nothwendig, daß fie lange auf dem Rücken_liegen bleibe, da die Mutter

short time, and immediately shuts it up very closely. It is lawful for a young girl, who is forced, to turn herself, and to endeavor, that she may not receive the seed, because the injury falls upon her; but it is not lawful to expel the seed once received, because now it has peaceful possession, and it cannot be ejected without an injury to nature.

den Samen schnell anzieht und bald sehr fest verschließt. Einem gezwungenen Mädchen ist erlaubt, sich zu wenden, und es zu vermeiden, den Samen zu empfangen, weil ihr derselbe mit Unrecht beigebracht wird; aber sie darf den empfangenen Samen nicht ausschütten, weil sie denselben im friedlichen Besitz hat, und er ohne Beleidigung der Natur nicht ausgeworfen werden kann. (B. 3. S. 317.)

105. Conjuges senes plerumque coeunt absque culpa, licet contingat semen extra vas effundi, id enim per accidens fit ex infirmitate naturæ. Quod si vires adeo sint fractæ ut nulla sit seminandi intra vas spes, jam nequeunt jure conjugii uti.—T. III. p. 317.

105. Old married people, for the most part, have connection without fault, although it may happen that the seed may be spilled outside of the female vessel, for that happens by accident, through the infirmity of nature. For if their strength is so worn out, that there is no hope of sowing the seed within the vessel, they cannot now use the law of marriage. Vol. iii. p. 317.

105. Verheirathete alte Leute haben gewöhnlich Begattungen ohne Verschuldungen, obwohl es sich zuträgt, daß der Same ausserhalb des Gefäßes verschüttet wird, es geschieht nämlich zufällig aus Naturschwäche. Denn wenn ihre Kräfte so gebrochen sind, daß sie auf die Besamung innerhalb des Gefäßes keine Hoffnung mehr haben, so können sie die Rechte des Ehestandes nicht mer ausüben. (B. 3.S. 317.)

106. Tactus, aspectus, et verba turpia inter conjuges, directa ad copulam, permittuntur, quia veluti media sunt ad finem licitum adhibita. Hinc licet illis se invicem ita excitare ut copulam facilius perficiant. Quæ autem ad copulam non referuntur, et solius voluptatis causa fiunt, non excedunt

culpam venialem, si tactus per se non sit valde fœdus, et si non adsit periculum pollutionis. Equidem status conjugalis jure censetur hæc pleraque quodammodo cohonestare, et gravem auferre turpitudinem : secus plurimis scrupulisque foret obnoxius. "Et hoc," inquit S. Alphonsus, "etiamsi copula tunc ipsis esset vetita ob morbum, vel esset impossibilis ob impotentiam quæ supervenisset." (L. vi. 933.) Quod si quis voto castitatis se ligasset, tunc plane forent illa omnia mortalia. Si impedimentum copulæ proveniat ex affinitate vel cogatione spirituali, etiam tunc tactus hujusmodi excusari possunt a mortali, quum pœna legis sit strictæ interpretationis.—T. III. pp. 317–18.

106. Touch, looks and vile words in reference to copulating are permitted among married people, because they are the means of coming to a lawful end. Hence it is lawful for them so to mutually excite each other so that they may perform copulation more easily. But those which do not refer to copulation, and are done for the sake of the carnal pleasure alone, do not go beyond venial sin, if the touch in itself is not very filthy, and if the danger of pollution be not present. Indeed the conjugal state is supposed by right, in a manner, to render honorable nearly all of these acts and to take away their grievous turpitude, otherwise it would be liable to many dangers and doubts. "And this," says S. Alphonsus, " although the copulation then

106. Betaſtungen, oder Blicke und ſchmutzige Ausdrucke in Beziehung auf die Begattung ſind unter Eheleuten erlaubt, weil das gleichſam Mittel ſind, zu einem erlaubten Zwecke zu kommen. Darum iſt es ihnen erlaubt, ſich gegenzeitig in dieſer Weiſe aufzuregen, um die Begattung zu erleichtern. Aber wenn ſich dergleichen nicht auf die Begattung bezieht und blos aus Geilheit geſchieht, ſo überſchreiten ſie die Grenze der erläßlichen Sünde nicht, wenn nicht die Betaſtungen an und für ſich ſehr ſchmutzig ſind, und wenn nicht die Gefahr der Pollution vorhanden iſt. Allerdings wird angenommen, daß das eheliche Verhältniß alles derartige gewiſſermaßen ehrbar mache und das gehäßige der Sache entferne, andernfalls wurde dergleichen als ſehr gefährlich und zweifelhaft erſcheinen.

might be forbidden to them by disease, or it might be impossible on account of impotency which might come upon them."—Wheras, if any one should bind himself by a vow of chastity, then all these would evidently be mortal sins. If an impediment to copulation should happen from affinity, or spiritual kindred, then even touches of this kind may be excused from mortal (sin), since it is the punishment of law and of a close interpretation. (Vol. iii. pp. 317--18.)

"Und dieses", sagt S. Alphonsus, "wenn ihnen auch zu der Zeit wegen Krankheit die Begattung verboten sein mag, oder unmöglich wegen nachfolgender Unvermögenheit."(B. 6. N. 933.) Hat sich aber jemand durch das Gelübbe der Keuschheit gebunden, dann würden dergleichen Dinge Tobsünde sein. Wenn das Hinderniß der Begattung aus Verwandtschaft oder geistlicher Verbindung hervorgeht, so sind solche Betastungen von der Tobsünde zu entschuldigen, da die Strafe des Gesetzes streng auszulegen ist. (B. 3. SS. 317=18.)

107. Quando periculum pollutionis in se, vel in altero prævidetur, difficilius excusantur tactus hujusmodi a gravi peccato, præsertim si videantur inchoata quædam pollutio ("prout esset digitum morose admovere intra vas femineum.") S. Alphonsi judicium damus; "Puto probabilius dicendum, quod actus turpes inter conjuges cum periculo pollutionis, tam in petente quam in reddente, sunt mortalia : nisi habeantur, ut conjuges se excitent ad copulam proxime secuturam, quia cum ipsi ad copulam jus habeant, habent etiam jus ad tales actus, tametsi pollutio per accidens copulam præveniat. Actus vero pudicos etiam censeo esse mortalia, si fiant cum periculo pollutionis in se, vel in altero, casu quo habeantur ob solam voluptatem, vel etiam ob levem causam : secus si ob causam gravem, puta si aliquando adsit urgens causa ostendendi indicia affectus ad fovendum mutuum amorem, vel ut conjux avertat suscipionem ab altero, quod ipse sit erga aliam personam propensus. Probabiliter dicunt Sanchez, Bosius,

et Escobar: "in reddente, tactus etiam impudicos, nisi sint tales ut videantur inchoata pollutio, esse licitos, quamvis adsit periculum pollutionis in alterutro, quia tunc reddens dat operam rei licitæ, ad quam obligatur propter jus petentis, qui tametsi peccat, non tamen jus amittit, cum culpa se teneat ex parte personæ." (L. vi. n. 933.) Immittere pudenda in os uxoris etiam obiter, videtur peccatum mortale "tum quia in hoc actu ob calorem oris adest proximum periculum pollutionis, tum quia hæc per se videtur nova species luxuriæ contra naturam (dicta ab aliquibus *irrumnatio*)." [L. vi. n. 935.] —Vol. III. p. 318.

107. When the danger of pollution is foreseen in one's self or in another, these kind of touches are harder to be excused from a grievous sin, especially if there appears to be a certain pollution begun ("as when the finger is moved about nicely within the female vessel.") We give the judgment of S. Alphonsus; "I think it should be said more probably, that vile acts among married persons, with the danger of pollution, both in the one seeking, and in the one yielding, are mortal sins, unless they may be had (done) that the married persons may excite themselves for immediate copulation, because when they have a right to copulate, they have also the right to such acts, although pollution by accident may precede copulation. But I consider also that modest acts are mortal, if they

are done with the danger of pollution in one's self or in another, in the case in which they are used on account of carnal pleasure alone, or also for some trifling cause; otherwise if on account of an important cause, for instance, if at any time there is an urgent need to show indications of affection to excite mutual love, or that the husband may avert suspicion from another because he may be inclined towards another person. Sanchez, Bossius and Escobar more probably say, "In the person rendering the debt, even immodest touches are lawful, unless they are such as appear, pollution begun, although the danger of pollution in another is present, because then the one rendering (the duty) gives operation to a lawful act, to which there is an obligation on account of the right of asking, who, although he sins, nevertheless does not lose his right, since a fault may be found (se teneat) on the part of the person." To put the privy parts into the mouth of a wife by chance appears to be a mortal sin, "because then in this act, on account of the heat of the mouth, the danger of pollution is very near, because also this appears to be in itself a new kind of carnal excess against nature, called by some a

mag. Ich bin aber der Meinung, daß auch züchtige Handlungen, wenn sie bei dem einen oder dem andern mit der Gefahr der Pollution geschehen, Todsünde sind, im Falle dieselben blos aus Wollust gethan werden, oder aus geringfügigen Ursachen; dagegen anders värhält sich die Sache, wenn es aus wichtigen Ursachen geschieht, wenn z. B. dringende Nothwendigkeit vorhanden ist, Anzeichen von Gemüthsbewegung zu geben, um gegenseitige Liebe hervorzurufen, oder damit der Mann den Verdacht wegen einer andern Person vermeide, als ob er für eine Andere Neigung hätte. Mit Wahrscheinlichkeit sagen Sanchez, Bossius und Escobar: "Bei der Person, welche die eheliche Pflicht leistet, sind auch unmoralische Betastungen erlaubt, ausser wenn die beiderseitige Gefahr der beginnen den Pollution vorhanden ist, indem dann der die Pflicht leistende Gatte sich mit einer erlaubten Sache befaßt, zu der er verpflichtet ist durch die Rechtsanspruche des die Pflicht verlangenden andern Gatten, der, obwohl er sündige, deßwegen dennoch sein Recht nicht verliert, ob auch die Person zum Theil Schuld trägt." (B. 6. N. 933.) Die Schamtheile in den Mund der Frau stecken, gelegentlich, scheint Todsünde zu sein, indem bei diesem Act wegen der Wärme des Munds leicht Gefahr der Pol-

being sucked (irrumnation). Vol. III. p. 318.

lution entſteht, wie auch weil das an und für ſich ſchon als eine Art Luſternheit erſcheint, die unnatürlich iſt (wird auch von Einigen Wieder= käuen genannt). (B. 6. N. 935.)

' 108. Tactus turpes sui ipsius, conjuge absente, vix possunt carere periculo proximo pollutionis, ideoque plerumque damnantur peccati mortalis. "Ratio, tum quia conjux non habet jus per se in proprium corpus, sed tantum per accidens nempe tantum, ut possit se disponere ad copulam ; unde cum eopula tunc non sit possibilis, tactus cum seipso omnino ei sunt illiciti ; tum quia tactus pudendorum, quando fiunt morose, et cum commotione spirituum, per se tendunt ad pollutionem, suntque proxime connexi cum ejus periculo." [L. vi. n. 936.]—T. III. pp. 318–19.

108. Vile handlings of one's self, the partner being absent, can scarcely lack the proximate danger of pollution, and so for the most part are to be condemned as mortal sins.—The reason is because a married person has not a right (per se) in itself over his own body, but only by accident, indeed only (sed tantum per accidens nempe tantum), that he may dispose himself to copulation ; whence when copulation is not possible, touches with himself are altogether unlawful for him ; because that the handlings (tactus) of the privates, when they are done nicely, and with a disturbance of the spirits, in themselves tend to pollution, and are very in-

108. Schmutzige Betaſtungen der eigenen Perſon in der Abweſen= heit des andern Gatten ſind wegen der nahe liegenden Gefahr der Pol= lution daher auch als Todſünde zu verdammen. Der Grund iſt, weil ein Ehegatte für ſich ſelbſt kein Recht hat über ſeinen Körper, obwohl un= ter Umſtänden inſoweit, daß er ſich zur Begattung vorbereiten kann, daher, wenn die Begattung nicht möglich iſt, alle Betaſtungen der eigenen Perſon unerlaubt ſind, in= dem eine Betaſtung der Schamthei= le, wenn dieſelbe langſam und mit Gemüthsaufregung geſchieht, an und für ſich zur Pollution führt und mit der Gefahr derſelben verbunden iſt. (B. 6. N. 936.)

timately connected with the danger of it.

109. Conjuge absente, delectatio de copula cogitata non caret gravi periculo. "Si delectatio habeatur non solum cum commotione spirituum, sed etiam cum titillatione seu voluptate venerea, sentio cum Concina. . . . contra Sporer, eam non posse excusari a mortali, quia talis delectatio est proxime conjuncta cum periculo pollutionis. Secus vero puto dicendum, si absit illa voluptuosa titillatio quia tunc non est delectationi proxime adnexum periculum pollutionis, etiamis adsit commotio spirituum, et sic revera sentit Sanchez, cum ibi non excuset delectationem cum voluptate venera sed tantum (ut ait) cum commotione et alteratione partium absque pollutionis periculo. At quia talis commotio propinqua est illi titillationi voluptuosæ, ideo maxime hortandi sunt conjuges, ut abstineant ab hujusmodi delectatione morosa." (L. vi. n. 937.) Venia sit dictis.*

109. The husband or wife being absent, the delight from intended copulation is not devoid of great danger. "If delight may be had not only with a disturbance of the spirits (affections), but also with a tickling or venereal pleasure, I think with Concina, against Sporer, that she cannot be excused

109. Wenn der Gatte abwesend ist, so kann es nicht ohne große Gefahr geschehen, sich über das Begatten gedanken zu machen. Wenn das Ergötzen hieran nicht blos mit Gemüthsbewegungen verbunden ist, sondern auch mit Kitzel oder Geilheiten, so glaube ich mit Concina, . . . gegen Sporer, daß dassel-

* Inclytos scriptor De° Maistre de conjugii abusu hæc notavii, quæ ponderent oporet qui affectantes morum puritate m¹a scrutandis rebus matrimonii abhorrent : "Si nous pouvions apercevoir clairement tous les maux qui resultent des generations desordonees, et des innombrables profanations de la premiere loi du monde, nous reculerions d'horreur. Voila pourquoi la seule religion vraie est aussi la seule qui sans pouvoir tout dire a l' homme, se soit neanmoins emparee du marriage et l' ait soumit a de saintes ordonnances." Le Compte De Maistre, Soirees de Saint Petersbourg, 1 Entretien, p. 55.

from mortal sin, because such delight is intimately connected with the danger of pollution. I think we may truly say otherwise if that voluptuous tickling is absent, because then the danger of pollution is not very intimately connected with the delight, although there is a disturbance of the spirits, and this is indeed the opinion of Sanchez, since he does not there excuse the delight with venereal pleasure, but only (as he says) with a disturbance and alteration of the parts without the danger of pollution. But because such commotion is nearly allied to that voluptuoustickling, therefore married persons are to be exhorted especially that they abstain from this kind of delicate delight." Let there be pardon for the things spoken.

be von der Todsünde nicht entschuldigt werden könne, weil ein solches Ergötzen mit der Gefahr der Pollution nahe verbunden ist. Es kann daher, wie ich glaube, auch wirklich gesagt werden, daß, wenn jener wollüstige Kitzel fehlt, dann das Ergötzen mit der Gefahr der Pollution nicht verbunden sei, wenn auch Gemüthsbewegung stattfindet, und so glaubt auch in der That Sanches, indem er dann dieses Ergötzen nicht mit dem wollüstigen Vergnügen entschuldigt, sondern nur (wie er sagt) mit der Aufregung und Reizung der Theile ohne Gefahr der Pollution. Aber da eine solche Aufreizung jenem wollüstigen Kitzel nahe liegt, so sind die Ehegatten um so mehr zu ermahnen, von solchem morosen Vergnügen abzustehen. (B. 6. N. 937.) Mit Erlaubniß, so zu sagen.

VOLUME 1, PAGE 318.

§ *VII. De Luxuria.*

92.   Ex causa autem necessaria, vel utili, vel convenienti animæ aut corpori, si pollutio preventura prævideatur, quam quis tamen animo aversatur, nulla est culpa, nisi adsit consensus periculum. "Hinc etiam prævisa pollutione involuntaria, licet I. Parochis, et etiam aliis confessariis audire confessiones mulierum, ac legere tractatus de rebus turpibus; chirurgis aspicere ac tangere partes feminæ ægrotantis, ac

studere rebus medicis: licet quoque aliis alloqui, osculari, aut amplexari mulieres juxta morem patriæ, servire in balneis, et similia.—(Hæc pessime detorsit infelix redux ad hæreticos.) II. Licet alicui, qui magnum pruritum patitur in verendis, illum tactu abigere, etiamsi pollutio sequatur. Caute tamen abstinendum est, si puritus non sit valde molestus. III. Sic etiam licet, etiam prævisa pollutione, equitare causa utilitatis. IV. Licet decumbere aliquo situ ad commodius quiescendum. V. Cibos calidos aut potus moderate sumere, et honestas choreas ducre." (S. Alphonsus l. iii. n. 483.)

§ VII. Of Luxury.

92. If however it should be foreseen that pollution will ensue from some cause that is necessary, or useful, or advantageous to soul or body, although the mind should be adverse to it, there is no sin, so long as there is no danger of consenting to it. "Hence even though involuntary pollution should be foreseen, it is proper for 1. Parish Priests and also other confessors, to hear the confessions of women, and to read treatises on obscene subjects; to look on surgical operations and touch the parts of a sick woman and attend to medical studies; it is permitted also to others, to accost, kiss or embrace women, according to the custom of the country, to wait on them in bathing, and things of a similar character. 2. It is lawful for any one, who suffers great itch-

§ VII. Von wollüstiger Schwelgerei.

92 Wenn vorauszusehen ist, daß aus einer nothwendigen, oder nützlichen, der Seele oder dem Körper zuträglichen Ursache Pollution entsteht, obwohl man jedoch dagegen abgeneigt ist, so ist das keine Sünde, wenn man nicht in der Gefahr steht, Einwilligung dazu zu geben. "Daher, obwohl ohne die Absicht dazu, Pollution vorauszusehen, ist es erlaubt: 1. Einem Ortspriester, und auch andern Beichtvätern, die Beichte von Weibern anzuhören und über schmutzige Dinge Abhandlungen zu lesen, den Chirurgen bei Operationen zuzusehen und die Körpertheile von kranken Frauenspersonen zu berühren und medizinische Dinge zu studiren; ebenso ist es auch erlaubt, Andere anzureden, Weiber zu küssen und zu umarmen nach der Landessitte, beim Baden Dienste zu

ing in the privates, to relieve it by touching, although pollution may follow. Yet this must be cautiously avoided if the itching is not very troublesome. 3. So also, it is lawful to ride on horseback for a useful purpose, even though pollution should be foreseen. 4. It is lawful to lie in any position, in order to rest more conveniently. 5. To take warm food or drink, in moderation, and to lead in decent dances.

leiſten und dergleichen. 2. Es iſt jedem, der ſtarkes Jucken in dem Geſchlechtstheilen verſpürt, erlaubt, es durch Betaſten zu vertreiben, auch wenn Pollution darauf erfolgt. Es muß aber ſorgfältig vermieden werden, wenn das Jucken nicht ſehr heftig iſt. 3. So iſt auch das Reiten erlaubt, und wenn Pollution vorhergeſehen wird, wenn es aus Grunden des Nützlichkeit geſchieht. 4. Es iſt erlaubt, in irgend einer Lage zu liegen, um beſſer zu ruhen. 5. Warme Speiſen oder Getränke zu nehmen und ehrbare Tänze mitzumachen.

VOLUME 3, PAGE 172

De Sigillo Confessionis.

87. Interrogatus confessarius utrum quis apud eum confessus fuerit, poterit plerumque respondere, prout res se habet. Quod si clam accesserit, ipsam confessionem celatam volens, putant plures, et quidem recte, judice S. Alphonso, frangi sigillum si accessus ejus a confessario declaretur, nam gravioris, peccati suspicionem facile injicit. (L. vi. n. 638.) De iis autem quæ confitendo declarantur, nihil prorsus dicendum est; ea enim ignorare causetur; quum nonnisi Dei vices gerenti innotescant. "Homo non adducitur in testimonium, nisi ut homo. Et ideo sine læsione conscientiæ potest jurare se nescire, quod scit tantum ut Deus. (S. Thom. Suppl. iii. p. qu. xi. art. i. ad 3.) Igitur simpliciter denegare debet se ea nosse: quod si aliunde noverit, cavendum ne quid certius ex confessione proferatur.

The Seal of confession.   Das Beichtsiegel.

87. When a confessor is asked whether any one has confessed to him, he may generally reply as the case is. If he has come secretly, wishing the confession itself to be concealed, many think and rightly indeed, according to the opinion of S. Alphonsus, (Liguri,) that his seal is broken, if his application to him be mentioned by the confessor, for he may easily cause him to incur suspicion of a more than commonly grievous sin. Of the things which are declared in confession, nothing further is to be said; for he is supposed not to know them, when they are known only to the vicegerent of God. "A man is brought as a witness, only as a man. And therefore, without injury to conscience he can swear, that he does not know those things, which he knows only as God." Therefore he ought simply to deny that he knows these things, if he has learned them from another source, care must be taken lest anything should be reported more accurately from the confession.

87. Wenn ein Beichtvater gefragt wird, ob irgend ein gewisser ihm gebeichtet habe, so kann er gewöhlich antworten wie sich die Sache verhält. Wenn einer aber heimlich zu ihm gekommen ist, und es geheim gehalten haben möchte, daß er gebeichtet hat, so glauben Viele, und zwar mit Recht, nach der Meinung des S. Alphonso, daß das Siegel gebrochen worden, wenn der Zutritt desselben zum Beichtstuhl vom Beichtvater ausgesagt wird, indem er leicht damit den Verdacht einer größeren Sünde auf ihn wirft. (B. 6. N. 638.) Von dem, was in der Beichte mitgetheilt wurde, darf nichts weiter gesagt werden; denn man nimmt an, daß er es nicht wisse, indem Niemand, als der Stellvertreter Gottes es weiß. "Ein Mensch wird nicht anders zum Zeugnißgeben aufgefordert, denn als Mensch. Und daher kann er auch, ohne das Gewissen zu verletzen, schwören, daß er nichts wisse, da er es nur weiß als Gott." (S. Thom. Suppl. 3. bis 11. Art. 1. bis 3.) Er soll daher einfach es läugnen, daß er jene Dinge wisse. Wenn ihm di Sache von sonst irgend einer Seite her bekannt sein sollte, so muß er sich hüten, daß er etwas Gewisseres aus der Beichte angibt.